SAVING LARRY'S HAIRLINE

SCOTT ROSE & ERNIE BRANDON

SAVING LARRY'S HAIRLINE

A COMEDY ABOUT LOSING IT ALL

ISBN 979-8-9947026-0-4

Cover design by Damonza
Interior formatting by Scott Rose

Published by ScottWorld
2028 E. Ben White Blvd #240-2491
Austin, Texas 78741
USA
scottworld.com

Special thanks to
Bradley Rose,
a very well-haired man

1. Black Screen

We open on a black screen.

A quote fades in. It reads:

"I don't consider myself bald, I'm just taller than my hair." -Seneca (Roman philosopher, mid-1st century A.D.)

The quote fades to black.

FADE IN:

2. Int. Child's Bedroom - Morning

We slowly pan across a child's bedroom, which reveals memories everywhere.

There are school awards for punctuality, perfect attendance, and best computer lab assistant. There are trophies for spelling bee champ and mathlete of the year.

We see a summer camp photo of a group of boys around a campfire with their arms around each other.

As we continue to pan across the room, we see board games, comic books, and movie posters.

An older woman comes tiptoeing into the room with a stack of freshly folded laundry in her hands.

This woman is LARRY'S MOM.

She places the stack of laundry on a chair, and then she tiptoes towards a race car bed that is occupied by a large body that is hidden underneath the blankets.

The hidden body is LARRY.

Larry's mom says in a singsong voice:

LARRY'S MOM

Good morning, Larry! Rise and shine, my little bubala!

The body is startled awake. Larry's head hits the headboard while his feet hit the bottom of the bed at the same time.

LARRY

Owwww!

Larry sits up. We see that Larry is a fully grown man with a full head of hair. He is clearly too big for the race car bed.

LARRY'S MOM

Sweetie, it's the first day of November! Do you know what that means?

LARRY

Yeah, mom, it's Day of the Dead. Which is exactly how I feel inside.

LARRY'S MOM

No, silly! It's your birthday month! In just a few weeks, you'll be 40! Have you decided what you want for your birthday?

LARRY

Yeah! The same thing I've been telling you I want for the last 6 months. I want my wife back. I want to move back into my house. I want my old life back. I just want to be happy again.

LARRY'S MOM

Oh, Larry. You can be happy right now. You just need to take your Vitamin G! Vitamin gratitude!

LARRY

Mom, there is absolutely nothing that I can possibly be grateful for. I'm gonna be 40 years old and I'm all alone! I have nothing!

LARRY'S MOM

You have a good job. You have good friends. You even have a beautiful car.

LARRY

All I want is to get back together with Lydia.

Larry lifts up his left hand to show his mom his wedding ring.

LARRY'S MOM

Larry, it's time to take off your wedding ring. You need to move on. You should actually be grateful that that bitch left you.

LARRY

Mom! She's not a bitch! She's a really good person!

LARRY'S MOM

Okay, Larry, whatever you say. But there's one thing you have that you should be incredibly grateful for — so much so that every man on the planet would love to be in your shoes!

LARRY

Oh yeah? What's that?

LARRY'S MOM

You have a full head of hair! We didn't think that was gonna happen, did we, mister?!

She tussles his hair.

LARRY'S MOM

You beat the family curse!

LARRY

I know, mom. Every man in the family is bald except for me. I'm the only one with hair. Do we have to go through this again?

She grabs a framed photo off the wall.

LARRY'S MOM

Here you are with all of your relatives on your prom night.

The photo shows an entire line of smiling bald men, standing shoulder to shoulder with a young teenage Larry in the middle.

Larry is wearing a tuxedo, and he is the only man in the entire photo with hair.

LARRY

Mom, I know you love that photo, but that was the OTHER time my heart got broken. I never made it to prom because Susie Jorgensen canceled on me at the last minute! She got food poisoning, remember? And then, when I tried to console her on the phone, she broke up with me. She said that I was suffocating her with sympathy! It took me another 12 years before I finally found Lydia.

LARRY'S MOM

Well, you should be grateful that all your bald relatives were there to comfort you while you cried yourself to sleep.

LARRY

That's the takeaway here? More gratitude?

LARRY'S MOM

Of course, your crying was nothing compared to the wailing and the howling of every man in this family who lost his hair. You have no idea how cruel the world is to bald men. Now take a shower and come downstairs. I've got another group of single ladies coming to meet you this morning!

LARRY

Ah, perfect. Another speed dating event. Should I wear a sash that says "still has all of his hair"?

The doorbell rings.

LARRY'S MOM

They're here! Hurry up! And don't forget to put in your hair tonic!

Larry rolls his eyes as she runs out of the room.

DISSOLVE TO:

3. Int. Mom's Kitchen - Morning

There are 12 women squeezed into the kitchen, all chattering excitedly with each other while eating and drinking. It is standing room only.

There is a huge smorgasbord of food for the ladies: mimosas, orange juice, bagels, muffins, eggs and bacon.

Four more women come walking in through the back door of the kitchen. Larry's mom greets the new arrivals from across the room.

LARRY'S MOM
Helloooo, ladies! Come in, come in, I've got chopped liver, I've got gefilte fish, I've got shmear! Who wants some more mimosas?

A few women hold their glasses out to get refills. Larry's mom walks around the room, pouring mimosas for the ladies.

A BUSINESS WOMAN puts her hand over her glass.

BUSINESS WOMAN
Oh, come on, Lucille... are you trying to get me drunk?

LARRY'S MOM
Of course, dear! Now move that hand out of the way!

The business woman laughs and moves her hand. Larry's mom fills up her glass.

The doorbell rings.

LARRY'S MOM

Come in!

A woman in yoga clothing comes rushing in through the back door. She pushes her way through the crowd.

YOGA WOMAN

Sorry I'm late! I didn't miss the slideshow, did I?

LARRY'S MOM

You're right on time! Grab some shmear! I made it fresh!

DISSOLVE TO:

4. Int. Larry's Bathroom - Morning

Larry has finished showering and wraps a towel around his waist.

He grabs a bottle of hair tonic and looks at it.

He sighs, pours some of the tonic into his hand, and rubs it into his scalp.

CUT TO:

5. Int. Mom's Kitchen - Morning

Larry's mom walks behind the kitchen counter where her laptop is sitting.

She opens the lid of her laptop, and the screen lights up to reveal a slideshow presentation entitled "My Larry."

LARRY'S MOM

Good morning, ladies!

Larry's mom clinks her mimosa glass with a fork.

The women quiet down, and several women respond back.

VARIOUS WOMEN

- Good morning, Lucille!
- Good morning!

LARRY'S MOM

Ladies, I want to tell you all about my precious Larry!

Larry's mom advances to the next slide, which has a photo of Larry and his mom smiling at the camera.

LARRY'S MOM

This is Larry, my special little boy!

A few women respond.

VARIOUS WOMEN

- Awwwwww!
- So sweet!

Larry's mom advances to the next slide, which shows young Larry playing on a playground.

LARRY'S MOM
Look how cute he was in 1st grade! You could already tell what a handsome man he was going to be.

She advances to the next slide, which shows Larry holding a trophy onstage.

LARRY'S MOM
In 6th grade, Larry won the spelling bee championship. He's always been incredibly bright! And just wait until you hear about high school...

DISSOLVE TO:

6. Int. Staircase - Morning

Larry is walking down the stairs. He is dressed in office attire.

There are family photos on the walls of the staircase. All the men in all the photos are bald.

When Larry gets to the bottom landing of the stairs, he looks up at a gigantic framed photo of UNCLE LEROY, who is completely bald and sitting alone in a sparsely furnished apartment.

LARRY

Oh, Uncle Leroy... no hair, no money, no wife. But at least you get to rest in peace, you lucky bastard.

Larry walks offscreen.

CUT TO:

7. Int. Mom's Kitchen - Morning

The slideshow is on a final slide of adult Larry wearing a Christmas sweater and holding a glass of eggnog.

LARRY'S MOM

And that's my little Renaissance Man! Who wouldn't love a man like this? Ladies, there are women all over town who would kill to be with Larry! Trust me, when you know Larry, there are no other men.

The women give a round of applause.

Larry walks into the kitchen, and the women are instantly impressed. A few of them sit up straight and throw back their hair.

LARRY

Good morning, ladies. Has my mom convinced any of you that I'm a superhero yet?

LARRY'S MOM

You ARE my little superhero, Larry!

VARIOUS WOMEN

- Awwwwwwww.
- Soooo adorable!

LARRY

Well, nice to meet all... 20 of you?

The women laugh and wave hello to Larry.

VARIOUS WOMEN

- Hello, Larry!
- Nice to meet you!
- Your mom told us so much about you!

Larry grabs a bagel and takes a bite.

LARRY'S MOM

Oh, Larry! Look who's here! It's Hilda and Gwendolyn. I was telling you about them from pickleball. And this is Heather from yoga class. She runs her own marketing agency! Martha in the back there is a doctor! I met her at temple! And I'm sorry, dear, I don't remember your name.

FRAN

It's Fran.

LARRY'S MOM

Ah, yes, Fran from the book club. All the ladies from the book club, raise your hands!

Several women raise their hands.

LARRY'S MOM

Larry loves reading books!

Fran speaks up.

FRAN

What book are you reading now?

LARRY

Well, I mostly read computer manuals for work. I'm an I.T. guy.

FRAN

I'm out.

She gets up and walks towards the back door.

LARRY'S MOM
Wait! Dear! What's wrong?

FRAN
No offense, it's just not for me. My ex read technical manuals in his free time. He was so boring.

LARRY'S MOM
It's not as boring as it sounds! Larry is very enthralling when he's solving technical problems!

Fran walks out the back door. A few other women leave as well. The door slams shut behind them.

LARRY'S MOM
Never mind them, ladies. Larry, you remember Tina, right?

A quiet, sweet-looking girl waves hello to Larry.

TINA
Hi Larry. Nice to see you again.

LARRY
Oh, hi Tina. Weren't you here last week?

LARRY'S MOM
She's been here 3 times, Larry.

LARRY
Welcome back. I promise, I haven't improved.

Another woman speaks up.

WOMAN

Oh God, I already sense a strong connection between you two. I know when I'm out of the running.

She gets up and starts walking towards the back door.

LARRY'S MOM

What, already?!

The woman walks out the back door, and it slams shut behind her.

The woman in yoga clothes speaks up.

YOGA WOMAN

Lucille, thank you so much for doing this. It's so hard to meet good men these days. Larry, your mom is so wonderful. You must be so grateful.

Larry fakes a big smile.

LARRY

Sooo grateful.

The business woman is sitting at the kitchen table with a notebook. She is taking notes.

BUSINESS WOMAN

Larry, how long have you been employed?

LARRY

Ever since I graduated college?

BUSINESS WOMAN

No, this job.

LARRY

About 5 years?

BUSINESS WOMAN
What's your criminal record like?

LARRY'S MOM
My Larry!? With a criminal record?! Never!

BUSINESS WOMAN
How are his teeth?

LARRY'S MOM
They're perfect!

Larry's mom grabs Larry's mouth and shows off his teeth like she's showing off a horse.

BUSINESS WOMAN
Very nice.

LARRY'S MOM
Well, of course! What do you think? 2 years of braces, 6 years of retainer. No cavities, either.

From the back of the room, Hilda speaks up.

HILDA
So Larry, what do you do for fun?

LARRY
Well, I play board games with my friends every Friday night.

HILDA
Ewwww... board games? I'm out.

She stands up and starts walking towards the back door.

Gwendolyn gets up and walks towards the door as well.

GWENDOLYN
I'm out, too.

LARRY'S MOM

Wait, wait, wait, girls! Girls! These aren't just any board games — they're EUROPEAN board games!

HILDA

Yeah, I gotta go. But can I take some of your shmear home with me, Lucille?

LARRY'S MOM

No no no, ladies! Larry's a very fun person! He travels to Hawaii every year! He's got a timeshare!

GWENDOLYN

So it's the same trip every year?

LARRY'S MOM

Well yes, but it's guaranteed vacation! He HAS to travel to Hawaii.

GWENDOLYN

Yeah, I'd rather not know what every vacation is gonna look like for the rest of my life.

LARRY'S MOM

Well, if he gives them a year's notice, he can switch locations with somebody!

They both walk out the back door. The door slams shut behind them.

LARRY

It's okay. I'm not even on the market. I'm really sorry.

Larry holds up his hand to show his wedding ring. The yoga woman speaks up.

YOGA WOMAN
Wait, you're married?! What is this?

LARRY'S MOM
No no no. He's been divorced for 6 months now.

YOGA WOMAN
Been there, done that.

She walks out the back door, and several other women leave as well. The door slams shut behind them.

LARRY'S MOM
Wait! Come back! You didn't try the gefilte fish!

She holds up the plate of fish. The business woman looks around the room and starts sniffing.

BUSINESS WOMAN
Gross! What is that smell? Lucille, I think your gefilte fish is spoiled!

LARRY
No, sorry, it's me. It's my hair tonic.

All the women in the room gasp.

BUSINESS WOMAN
Oh my God, are you losing your hair? Lucille, does he have a hair problem?

LARRY'S MOM
No no no! No hair problems at all! The reason he HAS a full head of hair is because of the tonic! Larry's hairstylist says that he's going to have a full head of hair until the day he dies. He escaped the family curse!

BUSINESS WOMAN

Family curse? Yeah, that's a dealbreaker. I'm out of here.

She walks out the back door, and every woman follows her except for Tina.

LARRY'S MOM

No no no, he ESCAPED the curse!

The door slams shut behind them. Tina is the only woman remaining. She speaks up.

TINA

So that's it? I win?

LARRY

No, I'm sorry. I'm still in love with my ex-wife.

TINA

I know. I'm just kidding. It's pretty obvious you're still in love with her. I just like spending time with your mom. And she makes a really great shmear.

LARRY'S MOM

Oh well, Larry, we'll try again next week. Now don't forget your chinchilla hair jacket — it might be chilly today.

Larry's mom grabs a chinchilla hair jacket, and puts it on Larry. He looks terrible in it. There is chinchilla hair everywhere, and it's way too oversized — he's swimming in it. His face is buried in a fur collar, and the jacket extends all the way down to his knees.

LARRY

Mom, you know I hate this jacket.

LARRY'S MOM

Oh, stop it! Your grandfather's beautiful jacket from the old country?

Larry walks towards the back door and opens it.

LARRY'S MOM

Sweetie, don't forget your lunch!

She runs over and hands him a sack lunch. The sack is decorated with Larry's name and little red hearts on it.

LARRY

Great, now I'm ready for kindergarten AND a blizzard.

Larry walks out the back door. It slams shut behind him.

CUT TO:

8. Ext. Mom's Driveway - Morning

Larry takes a moment to collect himself. He takes a deep breath.

He starts walking towards his car, which is an upscale luxury sedan.

The next door neighbor, NEIGHBOR DAN, is taking down some Halloween decorations on his front lawn.

LARRY
Good morning, Dan.

NEIGHBOR DAN
Good morning, Larry. Wow, that's a — uh — interesting jacket you're wearing.

LARRY
I know, I hate this thing.

Larry takes off the chinchilla hair jacket, opens the back door of his car, and throws it into the backseat along with the sack lunch. He shuts the door.

NEIGHBOR DAN
I saw a lot of activity happening this morning!

LARRY
Yeah, my mom really wants me to start dating again.

NEIGHBOR DAN
So you're finally moving on from the bitch!

LARRY
She's not a bitch! I'm still trying to get back together with her.

Suddenly, Neighbor Dan's phone starts screeching loudly.

NEIGHBOR DAN
AHHHHHHHH! I hate these Amber Alerts!

LARRY
You can turn those off!

NEIGHBOR DAN
What?! No! How do you turn them off!

LARRY
Go into your settings!

Neighbor Dan follows Larry's instructions.

NEIGHBOR DAN
Okay!

LARRY
Tap on notifications!

NEIGHBOR DAN
Got it!

LARRY
Scroll all the way down to the bottom!

NEIGHBOR DAN
I'm scrolling!

LARRY
Keep scrolling!

NEIGHBOR DAN

Oh my God! There it is! Amber Alerts! Larry, you are so smart! How did you know that?

LARRY

Eh, I just read the manuals. It's my job. Speaking of which, I gotta get to work.

Larry gets into his car.

NEIGHBOR DAN

Thanks a million, Larry!

LARRY

You're welcome!

Larry closes the car door and drives off.

CUT TO:

9. Int./Ext. Larry's Car - Morning

Larry is driving through the city streets.

He presses play on the video screen in his car.

A beautiful, peaceful flute noise fills Larry's car, and the image of a man appears on the screen.

The man is an older Indian man with incredibly long, flowing, white hair. His eyes are closed and he appears to be meditating. He wears an ornate blue robe that is covered with sparkling blue diamonds. He is sitting on a pillow which is also encrusted with blue diamonds. He is in a pristine white room, and blue light is emanating off his body.

This man is BLUE DIAMOND. He speaks in a serene voice.

BLUE DIAMOND
Hello, my name is Blue Diamond.

LARRY
Hello, Blue Diamond.

BLUE DIAMOND
Thank you for being here. You are now on Lesson #42 of your meditation journey.

LARRY
I really need this today, Blue Diamond.

BLUE DIAMOND
Okay, now lean back and close your eyes.

LARRY

I can't close my eyes because I'm driving. I'm just gonna close one eye.

Larry closes one eye while continuing to drive.

BLUE DIAMOND

Think about what you're grateful for today.

LARRY

Are you kidding me? Nothing! My life's a mess!

BLUE DIAMOND

Very good, now take a deep breath and relax.

Larry takes a deep breath.

BLUE DIAMOND

Nothing's going on in your mind. Just pure stillness.

Larry is trying to relax while driving, but his one open eyeball keeps noticing things going by.

There is a wig store advertising "cheap wigs". A well-haired man walks proudly out of the store, and then a group of kids steal the wig off the man's head. He is completely bald. The kids point and laugh at his bald head. He covers his head in shame like he is covering his genitals. The kids go running off with his wig.

BLUE DIAMOND

Focus only on your breath. Let go of any thoughts.

Larry keeps driving, and his one open eyeball keeps noticing more things.

There is a billboard advertising hair surgery. The billboard is a moving billboard that has wooden planks of hair actively growing out of a wooden man's head. The billboard's slogan says, "Snip snip snip, poke poke poke, stitch stitch stitch. It's easy!"

BLUE DIAMOND

Big, deep breath in. Deep breath out.

Larry continues to take deep breaths while he drives, and his one open eyeball keeps getting distracted.

A man wearing a hat is riding a bicycle, and a gust of wind blows the hat off his head. He is completely bald. He tries to grab the hat as it flies through the air, but he falls off the bike and tumbles onto the dirty street.

BLUE DIAMOND

Release any thoughts that come into your mind. And remember, keep your eyes closed so you won't be distracted.

LARRY

Okay, but just for a few seconds at a time.

Larry closes both eyes for a second. Then he opens them to peek at the road. Then he closes them again.

BLUE DIAMOND

Breathe in. Breathe out.

Larry breathes deeply. He opens his eyes every few seconds to peek at the road, and then he closes them again.

BLUE DIAMOND

Focus on your breath.

Larry starts getting very relaxed, and he leaves his eyes shut for more than a few seconds.

BLUE DIAMOND

Very good. There are no distractions from your breath.

Larry finally opens his eyes.

He is about to run over an ANGRY HOMELESS GUY who is pushing a grocery cart across the middle of the street. The homeless guy is completely bald.

Larry screams and slams on his brakes.

LARRY

Holy shit!

Larry's car skids down the street towards the homeless guy, and it stops just inches before hitting him.

The homeless guy bangs his fist on Larry's hood, then holds up a sign which reads "Bald Lives Matter!"

Larry rolls down his window, and sticks his head out.

LARRY

What are you doing in the middle of the road?!

The homeless guy walks up to Larry's window.

ANGRY HOMELESS GUY

I'm really hungry, man. Do you have any money so I can buy some food?

LARRY

I don't have any money. Here, take this.

Larry grabs his sack lunch from the back seat and hands it to the homeless guy. The homeless guy rummages through the bag and sniffs it.

ANGRY HOMELESS GUY

What is this? It smells like eggs!

LARRY

It's an egg salad sandwich and a cup of yogurt. Enjoy.

ANGRY HOMELESS GUY

Bleccch! I'm allergic to eggs and yogurt! Why don't you give me money so I can buy what I want?

LARRY

Dude, I'm going through a rough time financially, okay?

The homeless guy pulls out the egg salad sandwich and smears it onto Larry's windshield.

LARRY

Come on, man! I would've eaten that!

ANGRY HOMELESS GUY

I need money!

LARRY

Sorry!

Larry starts driving off.

The homeless guy grabs the cup of yogurt and throws it at Larry's back windshield.

The yogurt explodes all over Larry's windshield, which startles Larry.

LARRY

What the hell?!

Larry's phone rings.

LARRY

Oh God, this better be good.

Larry answers the phone.

LARRY

Max! Did you find anything for me? I really need to get out of my mom's house.

MAX (O.S.)

Great news, Larry! I found the perfect place for you to rent! It's in the perfect location too — just one block from the lake!

LARRY

One block from the lake? Are you sure that's in my price range?

MAX (O.S.)

Yeah yeah yeah! This is totally in your budget. But you gotta come now! It's gonna go quick.

LARRY

It's gotta be now? I'm running late for work.

MAX (O.S.)

Right now. This thing is hot. Major activity around this place. We gotta beat out all the competition!

LARRY

Fine.

MAX (O.S.)

Great, I'll text you the address. Start heading towards the lake!

LARRY

Okay, I'm coming.

Larry hangs up the phone, and he looks at the image of Blue Diamond on the video screen.

LARRY

There you go, Blue Diamond. Finally, something to be grateful for.

Larry makes a U-turn on the busy street. Cars blare their horns at him. Larry shouts at the angry drivers.

LARRY

I know, I know!

DISSOLVE TO:

10. Ext. Beautiful Mansion - Morning

Larry pulls into the driveway of a beautiful mansion. There are very elaborate Halloween decorations on the front lawn.

Standing by the front door is MAX, a short chubby man in his 40's. His haircut is a very high and tight buzz cut.

Max is wearing overalls that have brown stains all over them. He is wearing a fanny pack, and he is trying to put on an ill-fitting blazer over his overalls.

Larry gets out of his car and takes in the magnificent sight of the home. He walks up to Max at the front door.

LARRY
Max, this place looks incredible. Are you sure I can afford this?

MAX
Yeah, yeah, yeah! Sorry, just getting into my real estate blazer! I just finished snaking out a clogged toilet up the street. That's what all these brown stains are. Don't worry, most of these stains aren't fresh. Thank God for low-flow toilets, am I right? Otherwise, I wouldn't have any work as a plumber!

LARRY
Plumber? I thought you were a realtor?

MAX
Sure! And a locksmith!

LARRY
How many jobs do you have?

Max pulls out a business card from his fanny pack and looks at it.

MAX
Ummm.... 17? I'm a major part of the gig economy. Oh wait, do I got the marijuana sales on here? 18!

Max hands his business card to Larry.

The business card says "Max The Clown" at the top, with a whole bunch of other jobs listed underneath it.

Larry reads the card.

LARRY
Max The Clown?

MAX
Yeah! I do it all! I do kid's parties, I do clowns, I do magic shows, I do plumbing, I do real estate, I do tax returns, I'm a mobile bartender, I'm a locksmith, I do chimney sweeps. Oh, oh, actually I forgot, let me see that card...

He grabs the card from Larry.

MAX
Oh no, I already added it. Guided fishing tours.

LARRY
Guided fishing tours? Where?

MAX
Anywhere you want to fish! Oh damn, wait a second, I gotta update this. This is old.

Max grabs a pen from his fanny pack. He scribbles something onto the card, and hands it back to Larry.

MAX
I do fireworks too. If you ever need fireworks, let me know.

LARRY
Yeah, okay, I'll keep you in mind.

MAX
Do you wanna buy some weed?

LARRY
No, I don't smoke weed.

MAX
Did I mention the tax returns?

LARRY
Yeah, you mentioned that.

MAX
Well, keep the card. In case you need anything.

LARRY
I need a place to live. Can I see the house?

MAX
Oh, yeah! I forgot all about that!

Max bends over, lifts up the doormat, and grabs a key from under the mat. He unlocks the door and then rushes Larry inside.

MAX
Get in, quick! And wipe your feet! Don't bring in any dirt!

Larry walks inside while Max stays outside on the doorstep.

Max looks around the neighborhood nervously. He bends over, lifts up the doormat, and drops the key underneath the mat again.

He walks inside and closes the door behind him.

CUT TO:

11. Int. Beautiful Mansion - Morning

The mansion is spectacular and stunning. There is a gigantic marble staircase with a crystal chandelier hanging over it. There are bronze statues, magnificent pieces of artwork, tapestries hanging on the walls, silk curtains draping the windows, and plush velvet furniture. A grand piano sits in the corner of the living room, right next to a fireplace with antique clocks on its mantelpiece.

LARRY

Holy crap, this is in my budget?!

MAX

Yeah, yeah, yeah, come on. Follow me. Let's go.

Larry follows Max through the mansion. Larry runs his fingers along the staircase railing, and looks up at the incredibly tall ceilings.

LARRY

I'm already sold!

MAX

Don't touch anything. Come on, keep walking.

They walk into a gigantic kitchen that has polished marble countertops. There are state-of-the-art stainless steel appliances, and gorgeous wooden cabinets.

LARRY

Marble countertops? This place is a gold mine!

MAX

Shhh... keep it down, Larry. Not so loud.

Larry whispers.

LARRY

It smells so good in here. It smells like pumpkin spice!

MAX

Yeah, yeah, it smells great. Come on, all the way through. All the way through, buddy. Come on.

Max opens the back door and holds it open for Larry.

Larry walks out the back door and Max follows him outside.

Max shuts the door behind them.

CUT TO:

12. Ext. Backyard - Morning

Larry and Max walk into the backyard.

MAX

Here we are, Larry. This is your place.

The camera pans to reveal a shed. A small, corrugated metal shed with a "For Rent" sign in front of it.

LARRY

What?! What's this?

MAX

Your new home!

Max opens the door to the shed and a large rat comes scurrying out.

The shed is filled with tools and equipment. There is a bag of fertilizer on the ground with a skull & crossbones on it. There are cobwebs everywhere. There is a sleeping bag in the corner.

LARRY

Wait — what about the main house?

MAX

No no no, that's off limits. You can't afford that. This is the place. You didn't give me a lot to work with, Larry.

LARRY

So I can't use the main house?

MAX

No no no, you can NEVER. They want absolute privacy. That's a big no-no. I think the guy's gotta gun.

LARRY

But this is a shed! The best I can afford in this town is a shed?

MAX

Well, you're not really paying for the apartment, Larry. You're paying for the view.

LARRY

What view?

Max points to the house.

MAX

I mean, look at that house. You're gonna wake up to that view every day! But you can never go inside.

LARRY

We just went through there! Did we just commit a crime?

MAX

What, are you gonna tell on me? Please, oh God Larry, please don't tell on me! I could lose my realtor's license!

LARRY

No, I'm not gonna tell on you.

MAX

Oh, thank you so much, Larry! Let me give you some weed for free.

Max starts rummaging through his fanny pack.

LARRY
No! I don't smoke weed! But why did you take me through the house? Now I feel even more terrible about my life!

MAX
It's just — 2 minutes a day — I just need to see the good life! I just need a little taste!

LARRY
Okay, well look, I'm not gonna live in a shed. I need to live in a real house.

MAX
You can't afford a real house! Not with that alimony you're paying. That bitch really did you in.

LARRY
Max, I never called her a bitch. I'm doing everything I can to win her back.

Larry shows Max his wedding ring.

MAX
Alright, well, I'm not even sure you can afford the shed anyways, because it's a little bit over your budget.

LARRY
So why'd you bring me out here then?

MAX
I thought maybe you could sell your car. That would give you some extra cash until you get back on your feet again.

LARRY

I'm not selling my car. I love my car. It's the only thing I have leftover from my old life.

MAX

Larry, trust me, this is great living. I should know, because guess what? I live right there!

Max points, and the camera pans to reveal another corrugated metal shed.

LARRY

You live in a shed?!

MAX

Yeah, we're gonna be neighbors, Larry! Which reminds me — if you see a sock on my door, don't come a knockin'.

LARRY

Where do you go to the bathroom?

MAX

Larry! I'm out in nature! Everywhere is my bathroom!

LARRY

What about toilet paper?

Max points at a garden hose.

MAX

There's a hose right there! Great water pressure, too. No government water flow restrictions on hoses.

LARRY

Let me guess — is that where you shower too?

MAX
Yep. We keep things simple around here, Larry.

Larry notices some graffiti that is spray painted on Max's shed. The graffiti says "I'll kill you, baldie!"

LARRY
Does that graffiti say "I'll kill you, baldie"?

MAX
Yeah, yeah, I think so.

LARRY
Who did this?

MAX
Ah, these kids. You know, fun gang kids around the area.

LARRY
Fun gang kids?

MAX
You know, kids, they have fun, they get in gangs. But if you catch one, call the cops. Don't try to take them on yourself.

LARRY
Who is baldie?

MAX
I'm not so sure, but I just use my spray-on hair just in case.

Max pulls out a can of spray-on hair from his fanny pack, and starts spraying hair particles onto his head.

Larry starts coughing.

LARRY
I didn't realize you were bald.

MAX
Yep, I use this spray to cover it up! They're little nano-fibers — they look just like real hairs! I just can't touch my head.

LARRY
What happens if you touch your head?

MAX
Well, then it looks like ants are crawling on me. You wanna touch?

LARRY
No, no, that's okay.

MAX
Yeah, touch it!

Max leans his head forward.

MAX
Come on! Put your hand on my head!

Larry carefully puts his hand on Max's head, and then removes it.

LARRY
Oh my God.

Max's head has a handprint on it, and Larry's hand is now covered with nano-fibers.

MAX
See? Ants! But if I don't touch my head, it looks great!

Max starts spraying his head again. Larry starts coughing.

MAX

Larry, you've got it all with that full head of hair. I'll never forget the night I found out I was going bald. You see that balcony up there?

Max points up at a balcony on the main house.

MAX

It all happened on a balcony much like that one. Of course, my balcony was much higher up. I was looking down at all you plebes from the penthouse suite of a 5-star hotel. I used to have it all. The world was my oyster cracker! I had beautiful hair. A curly blonde perm, went down to my shoulders. The babes couldn't keep their fingers off my hair. I didn't even have time to sign all the autographs that the chicks wanted from me. Oh Larry, I used to be part of the most famous band in North America. Well, the most famous band east of the Mississippi. Well, really in Florida. Actually, in South Florida. Well, really just in South Miami, but we played a few gigs in Key West. Everyone was sayin' we gotta sign him. Everyone was saying it. Well, everyone in my neighborhood. Well, it was actually my Uncle who said it. But my Uncle knew what the fuck he was talking about. I was living the dream, Larry. I was on top of the world. I was playing gigs, I was staying at 5-star hotels, I was banging chicks left and right. I used to get so much pussy you wouldn't believe it! The pussy was just waiting for me from the minute I got off stage. I used to do coke, pot, meth, shrooms, cat tranquilizers, freebase, Pine Sol, smokin' joints fulla carpet, whateva da fuck... where was I?

LARRY

Um... banging chicks left and right?

MAX

Right, so anyways, I'm up on my hotel balcony, freebasin' with this chick I picked up afta the show, and I'm completely outta my mind, and I'm naked, and I'm taking a hit off the crack pipe, and she starts making fun of me cuz she says I have a bald spot. This is the first time I heard of this. So I run into the bathroom, and I lock the door, and I start breaking off pieces of the mirror to look at the back of my head. And there it was. A shiny little bald spot, looking right back at me. I thought my life was over. So I start crying, and I won't come out of the bathroom, and I'm naked, and my hands are bleeding from the mirror, and I can't stop crying, and then finally I come out, and I walk onto the balcony and I'm bleeding, and I'm naked, and I'm crying, and I'm trying to suck another hit of crack cocaine off the pipe, and then all of a sudden, the next thing I know, I'm falling over the edge of the balcony.

He stops, and a realization comes over him.

MAX

Oh shit, I just realized now, I think that bitch tried to kill me! Because the last thing I remember, I was naked, and I was crying, and I was bleeding, and I was sucking on the crack pipe, and she was pushing me, and I was going over the rail... Oh shit, I think somehow when she was pushing me over the rail, that's how I ended up falling off the balcony! Because I was smoking on the crack pipe, and she was pushing me, and the next thing I knew I was falling over the edge. Wait a second, you know what? When she was pushing me over the rail, I think she was trying to kill me!

LARRY

Are you saying that the moment you started going bald, someone tried to kill you?

MAX

Yeah, my arm doesn't work so well ever since the accident. But I don't think it was an accident anymore. I just realized now, I think that chick was trying to kill me! Because the last thing I remember is, I was naked, and I was crying, and I was bleeding, and I was trying to suck a last hit of crack cocaine off the pipe, and she was pushing me, and I was going over the rail... Oh shit, when she was pushing me over the rail, that's how I ended up falling off the balcony!

Max stops and looks at Larry.

MAX

Good for you for gettin' divorced, man, cuz lemme tell you, these bitches, they will get you HIGH, and they will get you NAKED, and they will push you over the fucking RAIL! Anyway, that's when all this shit happened to my arm, and that pretty much ended my music career... and that pretty much ended the rest. All the money dried up, so I had to get a new gig. I started snaking people's toilets. Then I lost all my hair. And all the pussy dried up after that. Why did I start telling you this? I had a point...

LARRY

I have no idea.

MAX

Oh, right! The good news is that things worked out for me! Everything's fine, Larry! I thought my life was over, but my life wasn't over. I've got a pretty good life. I live in a really cool shed. I get to meet nice people like you. And I'm getting glasses next week so I can see again! So hang in there, Larry, and things will start looking up for you.

LARRY

That's, um... very inspiring. I gotta get to work.

Larry starts walking away. Max calls after him.

MAX

So you gonna rent the shed?

(beat)

Think about it!

DISSOLVE TO:

13. Int. Office Reception Area - Late Morning

Larry walks into an office building. He is now wearing an employee photo ID badge on a retractable chain around his neck.

A RECEPTIONIST is sitting at the front desk. There is a plastic orange pumpkin on the desk that is filled with Halloween candy.

The receptionist looks up when Larry walks in.

RECEPTIONIST
Oh Larry, thank God you're here! My email isn't working!

LARRY
Okay, let me see what's going on.

Larry walks around her desk, and starts typing on her keyboard.

An employee, MARTY, comes running up to the desk. He is also wearing an employee photo ID badge.

Marty is almost entirely bald, except for a ring of hair around the back of his head.

MARTY
Larry, where have you been?!

LARRY
Hey Marty. I know, I was just running a little late this morning.

MARTY

Mandatory meeting! Right now! All hands on deck!

LARRY

Nah, I never get invited to those meetings. I'm not important enough.

MARTY

Oh no, it's ALL hands on deck. It's everybody. The numbers are real bad this quarter. He's gonna fire people today.

LARRY

If it's all hands on deck, why aren't you in there?

MARTY

I'm trying to gather up my courage. I know he's gonna fire me! I'm gonna be the first one to go!

LARRY

What? Why would he fire you?

MARTY

Haven't you noticed? People like me don't last very long around here.

Marty points at his bald head.

LARRY

Come on, Marty. The world doesn't fire talented people just because they're missing some hair.

Suddenly, both Marty's phone and the receptionist's phone start screeching loudly.

MARTY
AHHHHHHHHH!

Marty holds his ears, wincing in pain. The receptionist yells over the noise.

RECEPTIONIST
Ohhhh God! I hate these Amber Alerts!

LARRY
You guys, you can turn those off!

RECEPTIONIST
No! Really?

MARTY
How?! How do we turn them off?!

LARRY
Go into your settings!

Marty and the receptionist follow Larry's instructions.

MARTY
All right!

RECEPTIONIST
I'm there!

LARRY
Okay, now tap on notifications!

MARTY
Notifications!

RECEPTIONIST
I'm there!

LARRY
Now scroll all the way to the bottom and
you'll see Amber Alerts!

MARTY
I don't see it!

LARRY
Keep scrolling!

RECEPTIONIST
Where is it?

LARRY
Keep scrolling!

MARTY
Holy cow! I just turned them off! I didn't even know that was possible!

RECEPTIONIST
Me too! Larry, you're a lifesaver! How do you know these things?

LARRY
Eh, I just read the manuals. It's my job. Your email is working now, too.

RECEPTIONIST
Ohhh, thank you!

LARRY
You're welcome.

MARTY
Alright, Larry, well you better get into that meeting right now.

LARRY
Okay, but you're coming with me.

MARTY
No, I can't. If I hide, I'll still have my job tomorrow.

LARRY
Come on, don't be ridiculous. If it's mandatory, you'll get fired for NOT going.

MARTY
You really think I'll be safe in there?

LARRY
Of course. Let's go.

CUT TO:

14. Int. Office Meeting Room - Late Morning

The meeting room is a large room packed with dozens of people. There are not enough seats for everybody. People are packed in against the walls, standing anywhere that there is room.

Everyone is silent to give their attention to the BOSS standing at the front of the room. The boss has a beautiful full head of hair — a gigantic blonde pompadour.

Marty and Larry quietly tip-toe into the room, trying not to disrupt the meeting.

Everyone immediately notices them. The boss is annoyed.

BOSS

Oh, here we go. Shirker #1 and shirker #2. Thank you for gracing us with your presence! Well, I was just about to explain to your cohorts here...

The boss is interrupted by a little person sitting next to him who starts clearing his throat and pointing at the paper in the boss' hand.

This little person is the HR GUY. He is dressed in a suit and tie, and he has a full head of hair.

HR GUY

Eh eh, eh eh eh....

BOSS

What, I gotta read this?

The boss looks down at the paper in his hand.

BOSS

These are the new HR rules?

The HR Guy nods his head yes.

HR GUY

Mm-hmm.

The boss starts reading the paper loudly to the room.

BOSS

Okay, before we start the meeting, I am required to acknowledge that we are having this meeting on the stolen ancestral tribal grounds of the Kawanapee — is that real? — the Kawanapee tribe. Who took it brutally from the Apache tribe, who raped & pillaged it from the Kukamanga tribe. We need to solemnly honor these stolen lands that we are meeting on.

The boss looks over at the HR Guy, who gives him a thumbs up.

HR GUY

Mm-hmm!

The boss crumples up the paper and tosses it into the trash.

BOSS

All right, so the new numbers came out today and we're not doing well. This is the first time we've been in the red. And with numbers this bad, somebody's gotta go. I gotta chase weakness out of this company. When I built this company, it had strength. Today's the day I clean out the weakness. At least one of you guys has gotta go, and if I can get my little HR guy onboard with me, then maybe I'll clear out the whole lot of you and start all over again from scratch!

He looks over at the HR guy. The HR guy holds up one finger.

HR GUY

Mm-mm.

BOSS

Awww... come on, maybe two? You're killing me here. Can you give me a second person?

The HR guy nods his head no.

HR GUY

Nuh-uh!

BOSS

I can't?! Why can't I?!

An EAGER EMPLOYEE speaks up.

EAGER EMPLOYEE

Excuse me, sir? If you're gonna fire somebody, maybe it should be the person who brings in the least amount of money for the company?

BOSS

I'm sorry, what?

EAGER EMPLOYEE

Well, sir, I just thought that if you really do need to fire someone, maybe we should just look at whoever brought in the least sales last quarter? I don't know, I'm just saying — maybe base it on merit?

BOSS

Sounds like racism to me. FIRED! FIRED FOR RACISM!

EAGER EMPLOYEE

What? What are you talking about?

BOSS

You want me to fire Carl?! A black man?!

The boss points at CARL, a black man.

Carl leans back smugly in his chair with his arms crossed and a broad smile on his face.

The boss growls.

BOSS

Are you trying to make this the whitest office in town?

EAGER EMPLOYEE

No! I didn't —

BOSS

Get out of here! Somebody throw him out the window! Security!

Two security guards who are standing in the corner rush forward and grab the employee.

The security guards are struggling to pick him up as he fights to get away from them.

EAGER EMPLOYEE

Ahhhhhhhh! LET ME GO!! I'm not a racist! I'm one of your best employees!

The security guards succeed at picking him up, and they carry him towards the window.

EAGER EMPLOYEE

I was your top seller last quarter!

A few employees open the window and beckon the security guards over.

The HR guy claps his hands enthusiastically.

HR GUY

Hee-hee!

BOSS

Somebody call the police to grab this crazy racist once he hits the ground!

The security guards are about to throw the employee out the window. They are swinging him and counting to three.

SECURITY GUARDS

One...

EAGER EMPLOYEE

Noooooo!!

SECURITY GUARDS

Two...

EAGER EMPLOYEE

Stop it!! I'm protected! I'm protected!

BOSS

Hold on!

The security guards stop swinging. The boss walks over.

BOSS

Yeah? Who you with?

EAGER EMPLOYEE

I'm gay! I'm with the gay community.

BOSS
Really? You're gay. Come on, what have you done? Because if it's just a little hand stuff —

He makes the handjob motion.

BOSS
— you're going out the window. Forget it.

EAGER EMPLOYEE
No no no, I — I've sucked a cock.

BOSS
Really? You've sucked a cock?

EAGER EMPLOYEE
Yes, I swear!

BOSS
All right, okay, leave him alone. Nobody would say that if they hadn't sucked a cock. Just — yuchhh.

The security guards put down the employee.

BOSS
So who are we gonna fire today?

A random employee speaks up.

RANDOM EMPLOYEE
Why don't you fire Ronnie? He hasn't been at work this entire week!

BOSS
No, we're not firing Ronnie. He's in the hospital. He fell off his unicycle into oncoming traffic. In fact, his family asked for our thoughts & prayers, and you know what? We're gonna come through for them.

I want 100% on these thoughts & prayers. Every single one of you! I want thoughts. And I want prayers. We don't have any stinking atheists in here, do we?

He looks at the HR guy.

BOSS

Do we?

The HR guy shrugs and makes the "I don't know" sound.

HR GUY

Mm-MM-mm!

BOSS

You're not allowed to ask them when you hire them?

HR GUY

Nuh-uh!

BOSS

(surprised)

Get out of here! Well is there a question you CAN ask them that's like that? Can you ask them where they think they're gonna go when they die? That's not the same thing, is it?

The HR guy nods yes.

HR GUY

Um-hmm!

BOSS

I love this little HR guy! All he does is follow me around and make sure I don't get sued!

The boss looks around the room.

BOSS
All right, you bums. I want each & every one of you on your knees, praying to Jesus.

The HR guy clears his throat and shakes his head no.

HR GUY
Nuh-uh! Nuh-uh!

BOSS
What? We can't talk about Jesus?

The HR guy shakes his head no.

HR GUY
Mmm-mm.

BOSS
How about the Torah?

HR GUY
Zsh zsh zsh zsh!

BOSS
Okay, well everybody pray to somebody. And none of this Kwanzaa bullshit, I heard about that, that's not real.

The employees start lowering their heads, closing their eyes, putting their hands together, and dropping to their knees.

BOSS
NOT NOW! ON YOUR OWN TIME!

Everybody opens their eyes and gets back in their seats.

BOSS
Okay, so who should I fire today?

Another employee speaks up.

ANOTHER EMPLOYEE
Two people came in late today!

BOSS
That's right! We have 2 shirkers amongst us who think it's okay to show up late!

Larry speaks up.

LARRY
I'm sorry, sir, I've been going through a rough time lately. I promise it won't happen again.

The boss makes the half-and-half sign with his hand.

BOSS
Yeah yeah, all right. A little tepid. But look at you. Look at that beautiful head of hair. You are definitely holding the line. How old are you?

LARRY
39?

BOSS
39 years old and that hairline is a wall. This is what I'm talking about, folks. This is strength. He's gonna be taking over this place someday.

The boss gets close to Larry's head, and starts sniffing.

BOSS
What is that? What is that fragrance?

LARRY
My shampoo? Lavender?

BOSS
No no no, that's the sweet smell of hair tonic. I love that smell. He's holding the line, folks! He does what it takes! He does what a man's supposed to do! You can learn a lot from a man like this! Did I call you shirker? This is the rare time I take it back. This is strength, people. You could all learn a lot from —

The boss pulls Larry's retractable photo ID badge towards himself.

BOSS
— Larry! Did I say you were late? You were just on time! Larry can do whatever he wants! Meeting starts when Larry gets here!

The boss lets go of the badge, and it snaps back onto Larry's chest.

BOSS
Round of applause for Larry holding the line!

The room applauds.

The boss walks over to Marty.

BOSS
Now as for you, Shirker #2. I don't recognize you. How long have you been here?

MARTY
It's me! Marty! I've been here for 20 years!

BOSS
Who? Marty?

MARTY
I used to be your boss! Remember?

BOSS

No...

MARTY

We're cousins!

BOSS

Marty?! With the golden locks of hair?? The long, beautiful, golden locks of hair?

MARTY

Yes, that's me!

BOSS

Noooo... that isn't you. That was a huge strapping man. Full of life. Gorgeous, flowing, luscious hair.

Marty pulls his retractable photo ID badge towards the boss.

The photo shows a much younger Marty with lots of beautiful blonde hair.

BOSS

Marty?! JESUS!! What the hell happened to you?!

Marty lets go of his badge and it snaps back onto his chest.

MARTY

Well, I got married, I had some kids, I got divorced, I got demoted a few times, a lot of stress, you know, getting older.

BOSS

Jesus, no wonder our marketing is such shit. I mean, does anybody even know the new shit anymore? I bet you're working on a fax machine out there. This is insane. No wonder we can't win. No no no, Marty, we can't have people looking like you around here. We need people to look sharp, young, healthy. You don't even look alive. No wonder we keep losing. You're a loser, Marty! I could get a guy fresh out of college who's half your age and half the price!

MARTY
I went to college! I'll work for half the price!

BOSS
See? I told you! Weakness! This is why we can't win! Ugh, look at you. How long have you been sneaking around my building like this? Customers see this? How long has it been like this?

MARTY
It's not that bad!

BOSS
Are you kidding me? Are you trying to bullshit me? You're gonna tell people that I fired you because you're bald. But I'm firing you because you're a liar. AND you're bald. You're a bald liar.

MARTY
I'm sorry, sir. Please don't fire me.

BOSS
This is what I always say about men who lose their hair. They turn from lions into lambs. They get old, they get weak, and we can push them over. It's like Samson! And Samson's in The Bible! So go fight with the Bible. You're not holding the line, Marty. This is why I need to have these meetings more often. It's like cockroaches. Once you

find one bald guy, you're bound to find
more bald guys scurrying around.

Something bumps into Larry's feet.

Larry looks down and sees a bald man lying on the ground, hiding from the boss.

The bald man looks up at Larry and says "Shhh..." by putting his finger up to his mouth.

Larry speaks up.

LARRY
Sir, I don't think you can fire a man just
because he's bald.

BOSS
I'm sorry, bald is not a protected class.

The boss looks at the HR guy, worried.

BOSS
Wait a second, I'm right about that, right?
They're not protected, are they?

The HR guy smiles and nods his head no.

HR GUY
Nuh-uh.

BOSS
I love this guy. I've got a little slice of
government in here. A little baby
government, he's so cute. I could just kiss
him.

The boss throws little air kisses towards the HR guy. The HR guy blushes and catches the air kisses.

BOSS
Let's all give a round of applause for our HR guy. This is the guy who turned our cafeteria vegan! Boiled kale, anyone? Who doesn't love the boiled kale! Round of applause everybody.

The room applauds, and the boss turns to Marty.

BOSS
Okay, you're fired! Go get your shit and get out. You're fired! Meeting's adjourned.

Everyone starts filing out of the meeting room.

Marty glares at Larry with anger.

MARTY
Thanks a lot for dragging me in here, Larry!

LARRY
I'm so sorry! I didn't know!

MARTY
Our friendship is over!

LARRY
No, don't say that. What about board games tonight?

MARTY
Board games canceled! Friendship canceled!

CUT TO:

15. Int. Office Bathroom - Late Morning

Inside the bathroom, there are several men nervously examining their heads in the bathroom mirror. All of them are in varying stages of baldness.

One man is adjusting his toupee in the mirror. Another guy pulls off his wig and dusts it off. Another guy is painting a hair-colored varnish onto his bald spot. One man is rubbing some cream into his scalp.

Another guy removes his hat to reveal a head filled with thinning hair.

HAT GUY

You see what happened in that meeting?
That's exactly why I wear this hat.

The toupee guy responds.

TOUPEE GUY

A hat is the dead giveaway that you're bald!

The wig guy puts his wig back onto his head.

WIG GUY

I'm still putting two kids through college.

He pats his wig.

WIG GUY

I just need this baby to get me through 3
more years.

Larry walks into the bathroom.

LARRY
I can't believe I got my friend fired. This would only happen to me.

HAT GUY
Nah, it's not your fault, Larry! I told Marty he should just hide.

CREAM GUY
Yeah, me too! Larry, you were with him! Didn't you tell him to stay out of the meeting?

LARRY
I didn't know what to say. I don't normally get called into those meetings.

TOUPEE GUY
Well, did you at least tell him NOT to stand right next to you with your full head of hair?!

LARRY
No! Should I have?

TOUPEE GUY
Yes! You got the hair surgery, didn't you?

LARRY
No, this is my real hair!

All the guys react.

GUYS
Nooooooooo!

TOUPEE GUY
That's unheard of! How does it feel to have all your own hair?

LARRY

I don't know, I guess I never thought it was that big of a deal until today.

The room goes nuts.

GUYS

- Not a big deal?!
- Are you crazy?
- It's everything!

LARRY

I mean, my mom always told me bald stories, but I never really believed them.

The toupee guy speaks up.

TOUPEE GUY

You think I would put this thing on my head for a fairy tale?

LARRY

Oh God, I think Marty hates me now.

One of the toilet stall doors swings open and bangs against the wall. The noise startles all the guys.

A pair of fancy black dress shoes walk out of the stall. The camera pans up to reveal perfectly crisp dress pants, suspenders, a blue dress shirt, a silk tie, and a beautifully chiseled face with an incredibly full head of slick black hair.

This is SLICK GUY. He gently smooths back his hair.

SLICK GUY

No, Larry. Marty doesn't hate you. Marty hates himself! Why else would anyone CHOOSE to go bald? How stupid do you have to be?

LARRY
Well, you can't really help it if you go bald.

SLICK GUY
Can't help it? Ohhhh, everybody, look at me, I have to go bald now! I don't feel sorry for that guy. I was telling him for a year to get the surgery already. It's his fault for getting fired.

The slick guy addresses the room.

SLICK GUY
Look at all you losers. You're kidding yourselves with your wigs and your pieces and your little bottles of paint. A real man doesn't go bald. A real man gets on a plane, goes to Istanbul, and gets the hair surgery!

The toupee guy responds.

TOUPEE GUY
Istanbul? Why not locally?

SLICK GUY
Istanbul's the cheapest. The fastest. No regulations. Not like here, with all of our government restrictions. It's like fucking China here. One wrong move and you're locked out of the system. Only the Turks get it. They won't give you a hard time, and they treat you like a goddamn king.

TOUPEE GUY
Did you get the surgery?

SLICK GUY

Of course I got the surgery! Look at me. I'm like Elvis 1958! My hair is bigger than my head! It's perfect! Why wouldn't you do it?

TOUPEE GUY

Well, it's still surgery. It's still someone cutting into my head.

SLICK GUY

Ooohh, I'm afwaid! They're gonna cut my widdle head open! Please, I had a cigarette and a glass of ouzo while they did it. They even gave me a fully baked chicken while I was sitting there.

TOUPEE GUY

I don't know, it just seems kinda risky.

SLICK GUY

What risk? Snip some hairs out of your ass, poke them through your scalp, and stitch it up. It's just like the commercial says: snip snip snip, poke poke poke, stitch stitch, stitch. It's easy!

TOUPEE GUY

I thought they take the hairs from your upper thigh?

SLICK GUY

Your ass IS your upper thigh! It goes from your butt to your head. For only 2,000 American dollars!

Larry speaks up.

LARRY

You let them put ass hairs into your head?

SLICK GUY
Who cares where they take it from, as long as it sticks!

LARRY
Are you sure that's sanitary?

SLICK GUY
Larry, they wash all the shit out of it. Come here, smell my hair.

He pulls Larry's face into his head.

SLICK GUY
You don't smell shit, do you?

LARRY
No. No shit.

The cream guy interrupts.

CREAM GUY
I'm gonna turn this around without surgery. I've got a plan.

He holds up his bottle of cream.

SLICK GUY
Plan? There is no plan for this! Do you think a billion losers would be bald if there was a plan? I'm telling you what the plan is. You get yourself on a plane to Istanbul. All new hair follicles. From your butt to your head. No shame!

CREAM GUY
I'm just saying, how hard can it be to grow back hair?

SLICK GUY
Have you ever seen a man regrow his hair?

CREAM GUY
Well, um...

SLICK GUY
How about you, Larry?

LARRY
Yeah, I think my cousin knew a guy who actually...

SLICK GUY
BULLSHIT! Have you met this guy?

LARRY
No?

SLICK GUY
It never happened, Larry. Nobody ever grows back their hair. Do you know why they call it male pattern baldness? Because the pattern is males go bald!

LARRY
So what's the big deal? Everyone's gonna run around scared about their hair because of one crazy boss?

SLICK GUY
One crazy boss?! Larry, you clearly don't understand the world we live in. This entire world is divided into two classes of people — the hairs and the hair nots. It's what defines everything in society. Bald men make 70 cents for every dollar that a haired man makes. Bald men are 8 times more likely to

end up in jail. Bald men have a 66% greater chance of dying before they're 40.

LARRY
(skeptical)
I haven't heard any of this before.

SLICK GUY
In fact, the only way that most men even realize they're balding is that society starts treating them differently. By the time they figure out that it's because of their hair, it's too late. Their lives are already in shambles. I know, because I was once in denial like these losers. You wanna see what happens when I call my ex-wife? The one who left me when I just started losing my hair?

The slick guy dials his phone, and puts it on speakerphone.

The phone starts ringing.

SLICK GUY
Oh sure, your wife might tell you to your face that it's not a big deal. But as soon as you walk out the door, she's sleeping with a guy with much better hair than you.

A woman picks up the phone and starts screaming.

WOMAN ON PHONE (V.O.)
Leave me alone, you bald idiot! I told you to lose my number, baldie!

She hangs up on him.

LARRY
Ouch, that's terrible.

SLICK GUY

Nah, it was the best thing that ever happened to me. Once I went to Istanbul and got this hair, I got all the ladies! They were coming out of the woodwork for me. I've got a whole harem of women now! I'm making kids all over the place and I don't even know how many I've got!

LARRY

Oh, is that good? Is that a good thing?

SLICK GUY

Yeah, it's fucking good! You're goddamn right it is! I'm repopulating the earth by myself! I'm the next Genghis Khan! Come on, Larry, you've got a great head of hair! How many ladies you got?

LARRY

Well, I'm primarily focused on getting my ex-wife back.

SLICK GUY

Are you sure you're not losing your hair? That might be why the bitch left you.

LARRY

Oh, she's not a bitch. She's actually very sweet.

SLICK GUY

Larry, listen to me. Even if you have a full head of hair right now, this can turn around on you in a day. So you need to listen to what I'm saying. If you even THINK you're going bald — if you even get a WHIFF that something's happening up there — you get your ass to Istanbul IMMEDIATELY and you get all of your hairs replaced before anyone even notices you have a problem. And don't just replace the hairs that have fallen out. You get ALL NEW HAIR. The full follicle replacement job. From your butt to your head.

LARRY

I highly doubt the world's gonna care if I start losing a few hairs.

SLICK GUY

Jesus, Larry. You still don't get it, do you? You've never really seen the world we're living in, have you? Boys, where do I need to take Larry to wake him up?

All the guys respond.

GUYS

The lunchroom!

SLICK GUY

Larry, once you see this, you'll never be able to unsee it. For the first time in your life, you're going to see the truth.

CUT TO:

16. Int. Office Lunchroom - Afternoon

Larry and the slick guy walk into the office lunchroom, which is buzzing with employees.

As they walk through the lunchroom, the slick guy narrates the activities happening around them.

SLICK GUY

Okay Larry, look over there. Have you ever noticed who sits together at the different tables? You got all the hair tables taking up most of the lunchroom, and then over there in the corner, all the hair not tables. We call that bald corner.

LARRY

So the bald people like sitting with each other. What's the big deal?

SLICK GUY

No Larry, they'd get their asses kicked if they tried to sit anywhere else. Watch this guy. He's getting a little too close to that hair table.

A bald guy is walking through the lunchroom with his lunch tray. He accidentally brushes up against a hair table.

Suddenly, all the haired guys stand up in anger. The bald guy drops his tray to the ground, and runs out of the lunchroom.

The haired guys laugh and high-five each other.

LARRY
Okay, I never noticed that before.

Larry points to bald corner.

LARRY
Hey, are there really that many bald men at the company? I don't remember seeing all those guys at the meeting.

SLICK GUY
Oh, they were there alright. But they've got all sorts of bald tricks so nobody sees them. They hide in the shadows. They crouch behind taller people. They're always tying their shoes. You wouldn't believe it, but if you get down on the floor, there's always 4 or 5 guys slithering around like snakes.

LARRY
Yes, I saw one of them!

SLICK GUY
You saw the lowest of the low, Larry. A total coward. A slithering bald man.

They continue walking through the lunchroom.

SLICK GUY
Okay, now look at the cashier. Watch carefully.

A guy with a full head of hair grabs a blueberry muffin from the counter, and shows it to the cashier.

The cashier nods at him that it's okay to pass.

SLICK GUY
Free muffin for the hair. Now watch the next guy. The hair not.

A bald guy notices that the previous guy didn't pay, so he grabs a blueberry muffin from the counter, shows it to the cashier, and starts to walk past her.

CASHIER
Hey! Where you going with that? You just gonna steal?

BALD LUNCHROOM GUY #1
No no no! I was just —

The cashier blows a whistle hanging around her neck.

CASHIER
Thief! Thief!

Two security guards rush over, grab the bald guy, and drag him away. The muffin falls to the ground.

LARRY
But he was just doing what the other guy did!

SLICK GUY
Yeah yeah, boo hoo. Now look at the next guy in line.

A well-haired guy walks up to the cashier with his food.

SLICK GUY
Normal head of hair. He's gonna pay for his food. But watch the cashier's fingers.

The cashier's fingers hit a few buttons on the cash register.

SLICK GUY
She totaled up his meal, but she never hit the tax button. He just got a tax-free meal! Now here comes a hair not.

A mostly-balding guy walks up to the cashier with his food.

SLICK GUY
Watch her fingers, Larry.

The cashier's finger hits the tax button twice.

LARRY
Did she just hit the tax button twice? She DOUBLE TAXED HIM for not having hair?

SLICK GUY
Someone's gotta pay for the hairs, right?

The slick guy leads Larry towards the lunch line.

SLICK GUY
Take a look at the lunch line. See the lady bringing out the hot french fries? She's putting them behind the older, colder french fries. That's because she's supposed to finish serving the old ones first. Let's see what happens.

A guy with a full head of hair walks up with his tray.

The french fry lady uses her tongs to serve him the hot french fries from the back.

LARRY
She just took from the back!

SLICK GUY
That's right. When you have hair, you always get the hot fresh ones. Now let's see what happens with baldie over here.

A bald guy walks up with his tray.

The french fry lady uses her tongs to serve him the cold french fries from the front.

The bald guy speaks up.

BALD LUNCHROOM GUY #2
Excuse me, can I please get the fries from the back? The hot ones?

FRENCH FRY LADY
You got enough. Other people need to eat too.

BALD LUNCHROOM GUY #2
No, I know. I just wanted the hot ones.

FRENCH FRY LADY
Your fries aren't getting any hotter with you standing there.

BALD LUNCHROOM GUY #2
But I just saw...

She reaches for the whistle around her neck.

FRENCH FRY LADY
You want no fries at all?

BALD LUNCHROOM GUY #2
No, no, thank you...

The bald guy droops and walks away with his tray of cold fries.

LARRY
But that's not fair!

SLICK GUY
Oh Larry, it's even more unfair than you realize. Bald people can only taste half their food to begin with. So the temperature of their food means everything to them!

LARRY
Bald people can only taste half their food?

SLICK GUY

Yep. When the hair goes, the tastebuds go as well. Check out soda lady over there. She knows this. She'll deprive the bald men of their ice.

The soda lady is filling up a glass of soda for a bald guy.

BALD LUNCHROOM GUY #3

Oh, could you please put some ice in my drink?

SODA LADY

Sorry, ice shortage.

She hands him the iceless glass of soda. He reluctantly takes it and walks away.

LARRY

She just gave him a warm glass of soda? That's inhumane!

SLICK GUY

There's bald discrimination everywhere, Larry. Once you open your eyes, you'll see it all around you.

Larry looks around the room.

The camera spins around the lunchroom from Larry's point of view, which reveals bald discrimination everywhere.

A well-haired man gets up from a chair massage. As soon as a bald guy sits down for a massage, the masseuse flips her sign to "Closed" and walks away.

A bald man walks up to a karaoke machine and picks up the microphone. A janitor unplugs the machine and rolls it away, grabbing the microphone as he leaves.

A bald guy smiles and tips his hat to a woman walking by. She slaps his face and continues walking.

A bald man is admiring a piece of artwork hanging on the wall. The artist flips the piece around so the bald man can't look at it.

The camera spins back to Larry's face.

LARRY
Unbelievable.

A bald guy walks up to Larry.

BALD LUNCHROOM GUY #4
Larry, how could you hang out with that fraud? He used to be one of us. Now he's just a bald traitor.

The slick guy responds.

SLICK GUY
It's shameful to be jealous of men who pick themselves up by their bootstraps.

BALD LUNCHROOM GUY #4
You're still bald under that hair! I'm real!

The bald guy storms off.

Just then, a hush falls over the lunchroom as a tall, handsome man is escorted into the room by security guards.

The man is wearing a tracksuit and has an extraordinarily long mane of straight black hair that flows all the way down to his thighs.

In slow motion, he walks into the room and flips back his hair.

Everyone in the lunchroom stops what they are doing to look at the man. A large number of people jump up from their seats to follow him as he walks. Several people whip out their phones to record his every move.

The slick guy is excited.

SLICK GUY

Oh wow! This is a very special day, Larry. I didn't know we were gonna get a sighting of celebrity hair today. This is a rare treat.

LARRY

Celebrity hair?

SLICK GUY

You've got your hairs and your hair nots, but there's a whole other level to this game. This is celebrity hair. You can't buy celebrity hair. You're either born with it or you're not.

The security guards lead the celebrity hair guy to a fancy table in the corner that is adorned with a tablecloth, candles, fine china, polished silverware, and a vase of roses. The man sits down in a plush velvet chair.

A chef walks over to the table, carrying a silver tray with a domed cover on it. He places the silver tray on the table and removes the lid to reveal a fully baked chicken.

SLICK GUY

A fully baked chicken. The ultimate status symbol.

A random person shouts from the crowd.

RANDOM PERSON

Hey, how come he gets meat?

SLICK GUY

Shhh... don't scare him away! Larry, when you have celebrity hair, you enter the realm of the gods. You get free meals, free clothes, free cars, and you even get your very own endorsement deals. Having celebrity hair is better than being a celebrity.

A bald guy runs over to the table to take a closeup photo, but he trips and falls.

A security guard angrily grabs a red velvet curtain and pulls it around the celebrity hair guy's table to give him privacy.

The crowd reacts.

CROWD
Awwwwwwwwww!!

SLICK GUY
Nice job, Stanley. It takes months to get a sighting like that. Amateur!

Suddenly, the boss walks into the lunchroom with the HR guy.

The bald men scurry to hide underneath tables and duck behind furniture. A few bald men drop to the floor and start sliding on their bellies.

Larry looks down and sees a bald man slithering at his feet.

The man looks up at Larry and hisses.

SLITHERING BALD MAN
Don't judge, Larry! This is called dignity!

CUT TO:

17. Int. Larry's Car - Afternoon

Larry is sitting in his car in the parking lot of the office.

He starts his car. The meditation flute sound plays, and Blue Diamond appears on the video screen.

BLUE DIAMOND
Another perfect day. Not a worry in the world.

LARRY
I'm sorry, Blue Diamond, I gotta make a call.

Larry pauses the video, and dials his phone.

The phone rings, and then a man picks up the phone.

MAN ON PHONE (O.S.)
Larry? Is everything okay?

LARRY
Sorry to bother you, but I was just wondering if there's any way you could squeeze me in for a quick session today? I just need a professional to tell me that everything's okay. You know, I just need some perspective.

We reveal that Larry is talking to a hairstylist in a hair salon, who has his phone on his shoulder while he's cutting someone's hair.

HAIRSTYLIST
Why, of course, Larry! Anything for you! You're my oldest and most loyal client!

Larry lets out a big sigh of relief.

LARRY

Oh, thank you so much. I'm feeling better already.

DISSOLVE TO:

18. Int. Hair Salon - Late Afternoon

Larry is sitting in a hairstyling chair at a busy upscale hair salon filled with trendy stylists and young, attractive customers.

Larry's HAIRSTYLIST is an effeminate man who has a full head of wavy golden hair.

LARRY

Thanks again for seeing me on such short notice.

The hairstylist is rifling his fingers through Larry's hair.

HAIRSTYLIST

Of course, Larry! We're practically family! Now what seems to be troubling you, dear?

LARRY

I just need a quick checkup. I don't really think there's a problem, but I've had such a crazy day that I just need to make sure everything's okay. This guy at work was saying that if there's even a hint of a problem then I need to take action immediately.

HAIRSTYLIST

Larry, Larry, Larry. What have I always told you?

LARRY

I'm gonna have a full head of hair until the day I die.

HAIRSTYLIST

That's right, Larry. You're going to be a beautiful corpse.

The hairstylist is combing Larry's hair and analyzing Larry's scalp.

LARRY

I know I'm fine. I've done everything you've told me to do. It's just that my life is such a disaster right now, so I wanted to rule this out as the cause. I saw my friend get fired today for being bald, so I figured I better just stay one step ahead of everything.

HAIRSTYLIST

You saw what? A guy got fired?

LARRY

Yeah, it was a weird meeting. It even devolved into whether I was holding the line.

HAIRSTYLIST

Well you are holding the line, Larry. Rest assured.

LARRY

I knew it. This was just a big waste of time.

The hairstylist suddenly stops and moves his face closer to Larry's scalp.

HAIRSTYLIST

Huh. Interesting.

LARRY

Interesting? What do you mean interesting?

HAIRSTYLIST

Uh-oh.

LARRY
What do you mean uh-oh? What's going on?

HAIRSTYLIST
I need silence, Larry! Silence!

LARRY
I'm still holding the line, right?

The hairstylist is frantically parting Larry's hair in the back and closely examining Larry's scalp.

HAIRSTYLIST
Could somebody get me a broom please? A hair broom? I need a broom and some lights!

LARRY
Please tell me what's happening.

HAIRSTYLIST
Stop panicking! Nobody panic! Everybody stop panicking!

LARRY
I think I'm starting to panic.

HAIRSTYLIST
There seems to be something missing here.

LARRY
Oh my God. Am I going bald?!

The entire salon becomes silent and everybody looks at Larry. There are a few gasps of horror in the background. Another stylist drops his scissors on the ground.

The hairstylist nervously tries to calm everyone down.

HAIRSTYLIST

(to the room)

HA HA HAAAA! He's only joking, folks! We don't say the "B" word around here!

LARRY

What word do we say then? Am I going that?

HAIRSTYLIST

(to the room)

Just a little gray hair, everybody! Nothing to see here! Back to normal! Back to one!

LARRY

Oh, so it's just a grey hair?

HAIRSTYLIST

No, Larry. Of course not. A grey hair would be charming. There's nothing charming about this.

LARRY

So what is it? I'm not losing my hair, am I?!

HAIRSTYLIST

I'm sorry, Larry, I thought this day would never come. You're officially pre-bald.

LARRY

Pre-bald!?

HAIRSTYLIST

You've lost your first follicle.

LARRY

No! That's impossible! I have a full head of hair! You just said I would be a beautiful corpse!

HAIRSTYLIST
Please keep it down, Larry!

LARRY
No no no no no! I can't be going bald!
Please, dear God, no! I need my hair! I
haven't even gotten my old life back yet!

The entire salon is staring at Larry.

HAIRSTYLIST
Larry, I'm sorry but I just need to knock you
out for a minute.

The hairstylist grabs a towel and pours some of his blue antiseptic liquid on it. He brings the towel towards Larry's face.

Before the towel reaches Larry, Larry faints on his own.

The screen fades to black as Larry goes unconscious.

FADE IN:

19. Int. Hair Supply Closet - Late Afternoon

Larry is sitting unconscious on a chair in a dark supply closet that is lit by a single lightbulb.

The hairstylist is slapping Larry's face.

HAIRSTYLIST

Larry! Larry!

Larry wakes up with a startle.

LARRY

Huh? Wha-? Where am I? Oh my God, is this your dungeon?

HAIRSTYLIST

Larry, listen to me. This is very important. We have to part ways from here on out. There's no nice way to tell you this, but you and me — we're done.

LARRY

What do you mean, we're done?

HAIRSTYLIST

Larry! I have an image to uphold here! I can't have bald guys shuffling around in here.

LARRY

But I still have a full head of hair, don't I? You said it's just one follicle, right?

HAIRSTYLIST

It's not just one follicle. It's one follicle TODAY. Tomorrow it's 2 follicles. The next day, it's 4. It's the beginning of the end, my boy. It may look like you have a full head of hair, but your follicles are no good anymore. Your entire head is like a field of dead wheat. Your hair is not firmly rooted anymore. Very soon, a simple sneeze will cause dozens of hairs to fly away. And soon after that, you'll be shedding like a mountain dog in summer.

LARRY

Do I have any chance of keeping my hair?

HAIRSTYLIST

Zero chance. It's a done deal. I'm sorry, Larry, but we all knew this day would come.

LARRY

What do you mean we all knew this day would come? You told me I would have a full head of hair until the day I die!

HAIRSTYLIST

Well, I was wrong Larry. It only goes in one direction now. Death.

LARRY

But after all these years? I did everything you said! I put on the hair tonic! I've been taking the vitamins! My diet is 50% soy!

HAIRSTYLIST

Yes, Larry, you were an excellent pupil.

LARRY
That's right! I would never leave anything to chance!

HAIRSTYLIST
Did you ever skip a day with the tonic?

LARRY
Only if I was running late.

HAIRSTYLIST
Then I guess you left something to chance, Larry.

LARRY
So it's my fault now?

HAIRSTYLIST
Well, it certainly isn't my fault! Did I tell you to put on the tonic or did I tell you to NOT put on the tonic?

LARRY
But I wasn't even going bald!

HAIRSTYLIST
Well good job, dummy, because now you are!

LARRY
Is there anything I can do to grow new hair?

HAIRSTYLIST
Impossible! Have you ever seen anybody grow new hair?

LARRY
Yes! I think my cousin knew a guy!

HAIRSTYLIST

Larry, if that ever happened in our society, I wouldn't have to get rid of customers like yourself every week.

LARRY

So what do we do now? There has to be something we can do!

HAIRSTYLIST

Don't rope me into this. There's no more "we" here. This is your problem now.

LARRY

Please! I really need your guidance.

The hairstylist grabs a book off a shelf and hands it to Larry.

HAIRSTYLIST

Take this, Larry. Let this guide you. It's a meditation book by a man named Blue Diamond.

LARRY

You already gave me this after my divorce! I even watch his meditation videos!

HAIRSTYLIST

Oh! Well then give it back to me! I need that copy!

He snatches the book back from Larry.

HAIRSTYLIST

Are you actually doing the meditations? Because you don't look very relaxed.

LARRY

Well no, I'm not relaxed! You just told me I'm going bald!

HAIRSTYLIST
That's true, Larry. Your life is over. Maybe now you can relax.

LARRY
There has to be a way to reverse this! I just need a plan! What's my plan?

HAIRSTYLIST
Larry, there's only one plan now. You need to quickly do everything in life that you've ever wanted to do with hair! If there's a vacation you've wanted to take, book it now. Because soon, hotels aren't going to have any more rooms available for you. If you've ever wanted a Rolex, buy it now, because the Swiss have zero tolerance for bald. If there's any foods you like, you better eat them now, because your tastebuds are gonna go shortly after your hair. Oh, and very important. Before it's too late, go ride in a convertible.

LARRY
A convertible? What good is that gonna do me?

HAIRSTYLIST
A bald man in a convertible? That's crazy! The whole point of a convertible is to feel the wind whipping through your hair!

LARRY
Okay, worst case scenario — how many years do I have left with my hair?

HAIRSTYLIST
Years?! Larry, you're not really understanding the timeline here.

The hairstylist pulls down a chart from a retractable roller mounted on the ceiling.

The chart shows drawings of men's heads that are progressing from a full head of hair to completely bald.

As the hairstylist speaks, he points to the increasingly bald heads on the chart.

HAIRSTYLIST
This is you today. In 3 months, you'll be here. You'll be training your own replacement at work.

LARRY
I'm already training a guy!

HAIRSTYLIST
In 6 months, you'll be here. Your own mother won't recognize you.

LARRY
Six months?!

The hairstylist points to the fully bald head.

HAIRSTYLIST
And in 12 months, you'll be here. You'll be lucky if you're homeless.

LARRY
I already can't afford a shed!

The hairstylist points at each balding head once again.

HAIRSTYLIST
3, 6, 12. Got it? 3, 6, 12. You're starting a process.

LARRY
I don't want to start a process! Abort! Abort the process!

HAIRSTYLIST
I'm sorry, Larry. You're a bald man walking.

LARRY
I'll get the surgery! I'll get the full follicle replacement!

HAIRSTYLIST
Surgery?! Larry! I'm fully against this idea! Chopping into your head isn't an option. Do you know how risky that is? Do you know how many people bleed to death from those operations?

LARRY
That guy at my work — he got the surgery and he looks great! He's Genghis Khan!

HAIRSTYLIST
For every one guy you know, I know 10. And their heads look like chopped up veal.

LARRY
No, I'm going to Istanbul! They're the best!

HAIRSTYLIST
Istanbul?! Oh my God, Larry. You'll be lucky if the man washed his hands before he cuts your head open! You're going to die of an infection to your head!

LARRY
So what do you want me to do? Slither around on the ground where nobody can see me?

HAIRSTYLIST

Yes, Larry. Grow old with dignity.

LARRY

No! I can't lose my hair! Not now! I need to get my old life back! I need to get the surgery!

HAIRSTYLIST

Larry, do you know what they do during the surgery?

LARRY

Yeah, it's snip snip snip, poke poke poke, stitch stitch stitch. It's easy!

HAIRSTYLIST

No, Larry. It's SNIP SNIP SNIP — they cut the hairs out of your ass. POKE POKE POKE — they peel your head back like a grape and they shove the hairs into your scalp. STITCH STITCH STITCH — they sew you back together like a rag doll. Does that sound easy to you?

LARRY

Easy enough!

HAIRSTYLIST

Fine, Larry! This goes against everything I stand for, but if you're going to get yourself killed at some filthy outhouse — if you're going to bleed to death on some Turkish table — the least I can do is send you someplace clean, someplace professional, someplace local. With proper regulations.

The hairstylist rummages through some papers on a shelf and pulls out a business card.

HAIRSTYLIST

This is my brother. He's a hair surgeon. You go see him. But whatever you do, do NOT tell him that I sent you.

LARRY

Why not?

HAIRSTYLIST

We haven't talked to each other in years. I don't want him knowing I'm thinking about him. I wouldn't give him the satisfaction.

The hairstylist hands the business card to Larry.

HAIRSTYLIST

Remember — you didn't get this from me.

LARRY

Got it. And after I get the surgery, everything will be back to normal again?

HAIRSTYLIST

Oh no, Larry. This is our last appointment. I don't cut shit hair.

LARRY

Well, maybe I can convince your brother to take it from my upper thigh?

HAIRSTYLIST

Your ass IS your upper thigh! No, Larry, you're dead to me. In the nicest way possible, you're dead to me. You and I live in two different worlds now. I live in a fabulous world of fabulous people with fabulous hair.

LARRY

And what world do I live in?

HAIRSTYLIST
The world where I show you the back door.

CUT TO:

20. Ext. Back Alley Behind Hair Salon - Late Afternoon

Larry walks out the back door of the hair salon into an alley. The hairstylist stays inside.

LARRY
I just need you to tell me that everything's gonna be okay.

The hairstylist slams the door in Larry's face.

Through the door, Larry hears a phone call being made on speakerphone.

PHONE OPERATOR (O.S.)
911, what's your emergency?

HAIRSTYLIST (O.S.)
Hello, there's a balding man acting strangely outside my business.

Larry covers his head with his hands, looks both ways, and scurries away.

CUT TO:

21. Int. Larry's Car - Early Evening

Larry is sitting in his car which is parked on the street.

He is in a daze, staring blankly at the world around him.

He sees a building for a plumbing company. On the window, there are big letters that read, "We'll attack your clogged drains until NO HAIR remains!"

He sees a billboard that says, "Save the Bald Eagle! Losing Mates. Disappearing Fast."

He notices another billboard advertising a beautiful island. It says, "Come visit Bald Head Island, North Carolina. Experience total isolation... just minutes from Cape Fear!"

Larry starts his car. The meditation flute sound plays, and Blue Diamond appears on the video screen.

BLUE DIAMOND

Don't we feel lucky to be alive? Feel your breath moving through your body — even through the hairs on your head!

Larry turns off the video.

He looks down at his phone and sees 11 missed calls from his mom.

He calls her back. The phone rings, and his mom picks up.

LARRY'S MOM (O.S.)

Larry! I've been so worried about you! Why aren't you home yet?

LARRY
I'm sorry, mom. I'm having a really bad day.

LARRY'S MOM (O.S.)
Oh no! What's wrong?

LARRY
I just got some really bad news.

LARRY'S MOM (O.S.)
Larry, you're scaring me! What happened? Is somebody dead? Who's dead?

LARRY
It's my head, mom. The family curse finally caught up with me.

LARRY'S MOM (O.S.)
What?! Larry?! Go talk to your hairstylist right now!

LARRY
I did. He's the one who told me. It's really happening.

LARRY'S MOM (O.S.)
Noooooooooooo!!! No no no no nooooooooooooooo!!! My Larry too!?! Oh God!! Why why why whyyyyyy? Why are you taking my sweet boy?!? Take me instead!!

LARRY
Mom, please stop. You're making it worse.

LARRY'S MOM (O.S.)
I knew this would happen! My nightmare is coming true! Waaaaaaaaaaaahhhhh!

LARRY
Okay mom, I gotta go. I'll call you later.

LARRY'S MOM (O.S.)
Get home right now, Larry! It's not safe for you out there! The world hates bald people!

Larry notices a hat store with dozens of hats in the display window.

LARRY
I'm sorry, mom. I can't come home right now. There's something I need to do.

LARRY'S MOM (O.S.)
Don't kill yourself, Larry! Life is too precious!

LARRY
I'm not gonna kill myself!

LARRY'S MOM (O.S.)
Are you holding a weapon? Put down the weapon!

LARRY
I'm not holding a weapon!

LARRY'S MOM (O.S.)
There's always a way out, Larry! Come home right now, and we'll figure something out! I'm going to stay on the line with you until you get home.

LARRY
No mom, I have to go. I know what I need to do.

Larry hangs up on his mom.

CUT TO:

22. Int. Mom's Kitchen - Early Evening

LARRY'S MOM

Oh my God! He hung up on me! He never hangs up on me!

She runs out the back door.

CUT TO:

23. Ext. Mom's Driveway - Early Evening

Neighbor Dan is doing some yard work on his front lawn.

Larry's mom bursts out of her house, practically falling down as she runs up to Neighbor Dan.

LARRY'S MOM
My son! Life! Over! Nightmare! Curse!

NEIGHBOR DAN
Lucille! Are you okay?

LARRY'S MOM
Please help! It's an emergency! Larry's in trouble! I need help!

NEIGHBOR DAN
Slow down, Lucille! What's happening?

LARRY'S MOM
LARRY'S GOING BALD!

She passes out on the lawn.

CUT TO:

24. Ext. Lydia's House - Early Evening

Larry drives his car speedily through a suburban neighborhood and parks crazily in front of a house. His car is halfway on the street and halfway on the driveway.

Larry gets out of the car. He is now wearing a ten-gallon cowboy hat.

Larry holds onto his hat as he goes running up to the front door of the house. The house is decorated for Halloween, including a full-sized skeleton sitting on the front porch.

Larry bangs on the door.

LARRY

Lydia! Please open up! I need to talk to you!

He rings the doorbell multiple times.

LARRY

Lydia! Please! It's important!

Larry looks over at the skeleton.

LARRY

Oh, what are you laughing at?

LYDIA opens the door. She is an attractive blonde woman wearing a bathrobe and holding a glass of wine.

LYDIA

Larry, why are you showing up unannounced? I told you to call first.

LARRY
Can I come inside?

LYDIA
No, Larry, this isn't your home anymore.

LARRY
I need to ask you a very important question.

LYDIA
Why are you wearing that ridiculous hat?

Lydia grabs the hat off his head and puts it on the skeleton.

LARRY
Did you leave me because you knew I was going bald?

LYDIA
Oh my God. What crazy ideas did your mother put into your head this time?

LARRY
It wasn't my mother. It was a professional. He told me that I'm pre-bald.

LYDIA
A professional? Do you mean your hairstylist? I told you not to see that narcissist anymore — he's just taking your money to sell you a bunch of smelly tonics that you don't need.

LARRY
Well, I'll have you know, that man stopped taking my money today. What does that tell you?

LYDIA
Your head is fine, Larry! Look!

She pulls on his hair to prove her point.

LARRY
Don't pull on it! I've got all loose follicles! They can fall out at any moment!

LYDIA
Larry! You have a full head of hair!

LARRY
That was before I saw my hairstylist! Now I have nothing! It's all dead wheat up there!

LYDIA
Wasn't your hairstylist the one who told you that you'd have hair until the day you die?

LARRY
Not anymore. Now it's 3, 6, 12, Lydia! 3, 6, 12! There's a whole timeline that you know nothing about — but believe me, it's terrible.

LYDIA
Larry, I don't have time for this right now. Alejandro's going to be here soon. I would really like your problems to not be my problems anymore. That IS what a divorce is.

LARRY
Just admit it! I think you've always seen a bald man when you looked at me. You would still be with me today if I had celebrity hair!

LYDIA
Celebrity hair? What the hell are you talking about? Larry, do you really think I'm that

shallow that I would leave you because of your hair?

LARRY
I think everybody's that shallow! After what I've seen today, I will never unsee it!

LYDIA
Larry, why are you still wearing your wedding ring? We talked about this. It's not healthy.

LARRY
I wear it because I'm optimistic about our future together.

LYDIA
We have no future together. How do you expect to meet another woman if you're advertising that you're still married?

LARRY
I don't want another woman! I want you!

Larry drops to his knees and clasps his hands together.

LYDIA
Oh my God, Larry. What are you doing?

LARRY
Please, Lydia. I'm begging you. Please remarry me. If it's about the hair, you don't have to worry because I'm getting it fixed. I'm getting all new hair follicles.

LYDIA
Please don't do anything foolish to your head. I promise you it won't make a difference.

LARRY

Lydia, I love you. You are my dream woman. I was living my dream life with you. This is our house! We built it together! We built an entire life together! All of my favorite memories are with you! My life is empty without you.

LYDIA

I'm building a new life with Alejandro now.

LARRY

No. Please don't say that. I want my life back.

LYDIA

This isn't your life anymore.

LARRY

Why? Why isn't it my life anymore?

LYDIA

Look, Larry, our relationship became dull and boring. It was great when I thought I wanted predictability and quiet nights playing board games with your friend Adam.

LARRY

His name's Alan.

LYDIA

Whatever, Larry. We're just not interested in the same things.

LARRY

I can change! I can learn to like the things you like! To LOVE the things you like!

LYDIA

Really? You're gonna start going to music festivals with me? You're gonna start playing tennis?

LARRY

Yes! Done!

LYDIA

How about weed? You seemed pretty horrified whenever I smoked weed.

LARRY

If that's what I need to do to save the marriage, let's light up a joint right now! Come on. Let's do it!

LYDIA

Larry, I'm looking for more adventure and excitement. I want a strong masculine man who's going to sweep me off my feet and throw me on the back of his motorcycle.

LARRY

You never told me you wanted a motorcycle! I would've bought one!

LYDIA

I need a man who leads ME into excitement!

LARRY

I can lead you!

(beat)

Where do you want me to lead you to?!

Lydia glares at him.

LARRY

Lydia, I can be exciting. Remember how much fun we had every year in Hawaii?

LYDIA

Yes, Larry. I remember. The same timeshare, the same activities on the same days. Snorkeling on Tuesday, volcano on Wednesday, luau on Thursday.

LARRY

But that was our special routine!

LYDIA

A routine can't be special. That's why it's called a routine.

LARRY

Okay, fine. You want to switch the luau to Wednesday?

LYDIA

No! I want something new and spontaneous!

LARRY

No problem! I can switch us to a different timeshare! I just need to give them a year's notice.

Lydia looks at Larry in disbelief as a loud motorcycle comes driving up the street.

The man driving the motorcycle has a difficult time navigating around Larry's crookedly parked car, so he gets off the motorcycle and walks it up Lydia's driveway.

Lydia is thrilled to see the man. She speaks in a singsong voice.

LYDIA

Alejandro's here!

ALEJANDRO parks the motorcycle and walks up to the front door. He is a buff Spanish man with rippling muscles and a long mane of black wavy hair. He has a deep, sultry voice with a heavy Spanish accent.

ALEJANDRO
Hola, mi amor.

Lydia jumps into Alejandro's arms. She gives him a deep French kiss while she runs her fingers through his long sexy hair.

From the ground on his knees, Larry speaks up.

LARRY
Um, excuse me? We were having a conversation here.

ALEJANDRO
Larry, this is not a good look for you. Come on, get up.

He puts out his hand. Larry reluctantly grabs his hand, and Alejandro pulls Larry up.

ALEJANDRO
A man must always have his feet firmly planted on the ground.

Alejandro helps Larry arrange his collar and starts brushing off Larry's pants.

LARRY
I can wipe my own knees.

ALEJANDRO
There you go. Good as new. Are you staying for dinner, Larry? I'm preparing a fantastic paella. I'm using a whole bottle of red wine.

LYDIA
No. Absolutely not. Larry was just leaving.

Lydia continues to run her fingers through Alejandro's hair.

LARRY
I'm sorry, Alejandro, but I'm here to get my wife back from you. No hard feelings. You've always been nice to me. No offense.

ALEJANDRO
None taken!
(to Lydia)
Do you want to be with Larry? I have no problem with it.

LARRY
Yes! Thank you!

LYDIA
No, I'd like to be with you, Alejandro.

ALEJANDRO
Larry, there is online dating. You can make a profile for yourself. I'll help you make one.

LARRY
I don't want to make a profile! I want my wife back!

Lydia keeps stroking Alejandro's hair.

ALEJANDRO
Larry, no man needs any particular woman. There are wonderful women everywhere. I can take out the garbage and meet 3 women along the way.

LARRY
Well, that's great. If it's so easy, then go get another woman at the garbage can!

Alejandro pulls Larry aside.

ALEJANDRO

Larry, this thing you are doing — it's not good for you. It's not how a man lives his life. There is just this one life, and we must live it to the fullest. Swing from the rafters. Dive from the highest point into the wildest river. Push the motorcycle to the farthest edges... faster, harder, stronger! Live, damn you, live! Like Hunter S. Thompson said, we should skid into our graves shouting "Wow! What a ride!"

LARRY

All of that sounds very dangerous.

ALEJANDRO

Exactly! Be dangerous!

LYDIA

Sweetie, can you make me a sangria?

ALEJANDRO

Certainly.

She grabs Alejandro and starts kissing him. She audibly purrs while she lovingly strokes his thick, flowing mane of hair.

Larry's eyes focus on Lydia's hands.

LARRY

Oh my God! It IS about his hair! You DID leave me because of my hair! He has MOUNTAINS of gorgeous hair! You can't keep your hands off his head! Tell me you wouldn't love me with hair like that.

Larry grabs Alejandro's hair and puts it onto his own head.

LARRY

If I looked like this, would we even be broken up?

ALEJANDRO

Ow! Ow!

LARRY

Do you find me exciting now? Am I more masculine?

Alejandro carefully pries Larry's fingers off his hair.

ALEJANDRO

Larry, that hurts!

LARRY

I'm not just gonna get all new hair. I'm gonna get MORE HAIR. I'm gonna get LONG, THICK, FLOWING, MASCULINE HAIR! I'm gonna cover myself in it like a shaggy coat. I'm gonna be an animal, Lydia, all for you! And you're gonna fall in love with me again! You'll see! I'm gonna snip snip snip, I'm gonna poke poke poke, and I'm gonna stitch stitch stitch! From my butt to my head! And I will be back here. WITH LONG FLOWING BLACK LOCKS OF SPANISH HAIR! And we will be back together again!

LYDIA

That's fine, Larry. Do whatever you want.

LARRY

You'll see, Lydia! You'll be back as soon as my hair's back! Say goodbye to bald Larry!

Larry turns around and marches towards his car, but his car is on the back of a tow truck.

LARRY

Hey! That's my car!

The tow truck drives away with Larry's car.

Larry turns around again to Lydia, where she is still standing in the doorway.

LARRY

Um, Lydia, can I have a —

She slams the door on him.

LARRY

— ride?

Larry stares at the door.

LARRY

Alejandro?

CUT TO:

25. Int. Mom's Living Room - Evening

Larry's mom is lying down on her couch. She has an icepack on her head and Neighbor Dan is standing over her.

LARRY'S MOM
Oh Dan, I'm so sorry that I don't have any food out for you. I've got some shmear in the refrigerator. Please, help yourself. I've got bagels in the pantry.

NEIGHBOR DAN
Lucille, calm down. You're in shock. Now tell me what happened. You said Larry's in trouble? He's going bald?

LARRY'S MOM
Yes! His hairstylist told him! The curse caught up to him!

NEIGHBOR DAN
Oh my God, this is awful. How did this happen to him so young?

LARRY'S MOM
I don't know! All that matters now is keeping him safe! I have no idea where he is, but we've gotta get him back home!

NEIGHBOR DAN
Are you telling me that his hairstylist gave him the news and then just let him walk out on his own? What sort of world do we live in where somebody does that?

LARRY'S MOM
We've gotta find him! We can't leave him alone out there.

NEIGHBOR DAN
Okay, how did he sound when you last spoke with him?

LARRY'S MOM
How do you think he sounded? He sounded like he had a gun to his mouth already! I tried to get him to come home, and then he hung up on me! I think he's gonna...

She draws a pantomime knife across her neck.

NEIGHBOR DAN
Jesus, Lucille. What are we waiting for?! We're losing light! He could already be dead in a gutter!

LARRY'S MOM
Oh, my Larry, my poor Larry!

NEIGHBOR DAN
Okay, I'll get more help. I've got the grandkids over. I'll round up the neighbors. I'll call my church too.

Neighbor Dan looks upwards and makes the sign of the cross on himself.

NEIGHBOR DAN
Dear God, wherever Larry is, may your mighty hand keep him and protect him!

CUT TO:

26. Ext. Car Towing Lot - Evening

The sky is beginning to get dark.

Larry gets into his car at a towing lot, and starts driving away.

The Blue Diamond meditation flute plays.

BLUE DIAMOND (O.S.)
What a relaxing day we've had.

DISSOLVE TO:

27. Ext. Drawbridge - Evening

Larry drives up a ramp to a Chicago-style drawbridge that extends over a lake, leading to downtown.

There is a tollbooth at the top of the ramp that has classical music playing inside.

The bridge operator, HERBIE, is sitting inside, enjoying the music. He has a full head of hair and a cheery disposition.

As Larry's car gets closer to the tollbooth, Herbie walks outside with one of his hands up.

HERBIE
Sorry, bridge is going up! Time to stop!

LARRY
No no no! I don't have 20 minutes to spare!

Herbie pulls a lever inside the booth. A warning buzzer goes off. Lights start flashing. A red and white striped "Danger" plank comes down in front of Larry's car to block the road.

The middle of the drawbridge road slowly splits in half and starts to go up to allow boats to pass underneath.

LARRY
Oh God, are you kidding me? I can't catch a break in my life!

Larry bangs his fist on the steering wheel.

HERBIE
Now hang on, mister, this bridge is a blessing!

LARRY

A blessing?! Really?! Is this some sort of a joke? Some big joke from the universe? Every time I try to do something in my life, the universe gets in my way and shuts me down! I don't have anything good in my life because the universe has done nothing but conspire against me! It won't even let me drive to see my friends tonight! Why do I even bother trying anymore? Well, I hear you universe, I get it! You hate me! Ha ha ha! Joke's on Larry! How about this? You win! I quit! I'm done! I'll go live in a shed and I'll go bald and I'll live a miserable lonely life until the day I die!

HERBIE

Whoa whoa whoa whoa whoa! What do you mean you're gonna live a miserable life? What do you mean you're gonna go bald? Why would you choose to go bald?

LARRY

Because I quit! I give up!

HERBIE

Now mister, I won't tolerate that type of talk on my bridge. That's not what this bridge is for! This isn't a bridge for quitters. How do you think that THIS side of the city would've gotten to THAT side of the city if they quit while making this bridge?! Now let's work on turning that frown upside-down.

LARRY

I'm sorry, I'm just feeling like the whole world's against me, and this bridge feels like more bad luck.

HERBIE

This bridge is actually good luck, because it brings people together! When it's down, it connects the people of uptown with the people of downtown. And when it's up, it gives us a chance to get to know each other! Let me introduce myself. My name's Herbie. Like the Love Bug!

He extends his hand towards Larry. They shake hands.

LARRY

Hi Herbie. I'm Larry. Nice to meet you.

HERBIE

Larry, I'm here to make sure that this is the best part of your day!

LARRY

You know, I can't remember the last time anybody ever said that to me.

HERBIE

Well, that's my job as a civil servant. It's what your taxes pay for!

Herbie taps Larry's headrest.

HERBIE

You know they call this a HEAD REST? Have there ever been 2 more beautiful words together? How often do you take advantage of your HEAD REST?

LARRY

I never use my headrest. I always drive with my head forward.

HERBIE

Like a caveman, Larry. Come on. Be civilized. Be good to yourself. Use your headrest.

Larry leans his head back against the headrest.

LARRY

That does feel nice.

HERBIE

Now lean back. When's the last time you leaned your seat all the way back?

LARRY

This goes further back?

Larry leans his seat all the way back.

LARRY

I had no idea! This is really comfortable.

HERBIE

Well, put your feet up on the dash!

LARRY

Really?

HERBIE

Come on!

Larry puts his feet on the dash.

LARRY

I could actually fall asleep like this.

HERBIE

Would you like a pillow for your feet?

LARRY

No, that's okay.

HERBIE

I didn't ask you to make everything okay, Larry. I asked you if you'd like a pillow for your feet!

LARRY

Oh! Okay, sure.

HERBIE

Larry, you don't even know what feels good anymore.

Herbie grabs a pillow from inside his booth and puts it under Larry's feet.

LARRY

You are so right. That feels incredible. You know, I've never even THOUGHT about putting a pillow under my feet, but aren't they the ones doing all the walking?

HERBIE

Now would you like something to eat?

LARRY

Well, I am a little hungry.

Herbie goes into the booth, turns up the classical music a little bit louder, and comes back with a platter of cheese.

HERBIE

Here's a little camembert. This one is aged cheddar. And this one is raw parmesan. Help yourself!

Larry takes a piece of cheese and puts it into his mouth.

LARRY

Mmmm... this is really good.

HERBIE

I'm heating up a nice cup of tea for you, too.

LARRY

That's very thoughtful!

HERBIE

Would you like me to blanket you with that beautiful coat you have in the backseat?

LARRY

My chinchilla hair jacket? Oh God, no! I hate that thing! It has more hair than I do! You can have it if you want!

HERBIE

No, no, I could never take that beautiful coat from you.

LARRY

Take it. It's yours.

HERBIE

No, really?

LARRY

I insist.

Herbie opens the back door, grabs the jacket, and puts it on.

He is swimming in chinchilla hair from his face down to his knees.

HERBIE

Oh, Larry, I love it! I can't thank you enough!

LARRY

It is my pleasure. Believe me.

HERBIE

Now tell me what's on your mind. What's been bothering you?

LARRY

Oh, it's a long story.

HERBIE

Well, that's what I'm here for! I guarantee you by the time that bridge comes down, we're going to have everything sorted out for you.

Herbie grabs a stool and sits down.

HERBIE

Start at the very beginning.

LARRY

Well, I guess if you want the whole story... it all started back in the old country. Two traders passing each other on a road. One of them accused the other one of selling poor quality grains, and he placed a curse on the other one. That man never had hair again. That was my great great great grandfather, and every man in his family has been cursed to be bald ever since...

TIME LAPSE.

Larry is sipping tea from a ceramic mug, and a bunch of strangers have gathered around his car.

LARRY

So I was working at the local computer shop. And that's where I met Lydia, the woman who would become the love of my life. One day, she walked in with her beautiful blonde hair...

TIME LAPSE.

More strangers have gathered around Larry's car.

LARRY

And when it was finally the night of our first date, she was running late and I was nervous that she wasn't gonna show...

TIME LAPSE.

Larry is standing outside his car now, talking to Herbie and all the strangers.

LARRY

And that was how I proposed to her, right there in the middle of the snowstorm...

TIME LAPSE.

LARRY

And I meant every vow on our wedding night. The happiest night of my life.

Larry holds up his hand to show his wedding ring. Herbie holds back a tear. The strangers are visibly moved.

TIME LAPSE.

LARRY

And that's the story of Alejandro! Can you believe it?

Herbie clutches his chest and his mouth drops open.

TIME LAPSE.

LARRY

And just when I thought things couldn't get any worse, I find out I'm pre-bald!

The strangers gasp.

TIME LAPSE.

LARRY

And that's when I met you, and all these lovely people on your bridge.

Herbie is wiping away his tears.

HERBIE

Oh my God, Larry, that's such a sad story. So tragic. This is a love story for the ages.

LARRY

I agree! It's an amazing love story! And she broke my heart!

HERBIE

Larry, take it from an expert. I hear these stories every day on my bridge, and your wife DEFINITELY left you because of your hair.

The strangers on the bridge emphatically agree.

STRANGERS

- Absolutely!
- It's so obvious!
- Without a doubt!

LARRY

I knew it!

HERBIE

You definitely can't quit now! You are so close to the finish line — it's such an easy fix!

LARRY

So I'm really gonna do the surgery?

Various strangers respond.

STRANGERS

- Yes, of course!
- You have to!
- It was the best decision of my life!

HERBIE

Larry, you have no time to waste. This is ZERO HOUR.

LARRY

It really is zero hour.

HERBIE

Larry, do you see that yacht that just passed under this bridge?

Herbie points to a gigantic yacht that has dozens of partying men and women on it. It even has a helicopter parked on its deck.

HERBIE

The guy who owns that yacht used to be bald as a bone. He used to wait here on my bridge in his car, crying to me about all his problems. I told him that he just needed to unleash his hair potential, and by God, he did. He got the hair surgery and it changed his life. And now? Now we wait for him.

The owner of the yacht is sitting in the captain's seat. He has a beautiful head of wavy brown hair with platinum blonde highlights.

He honks the yacht's horn and waves to Herbie. He shouts through a megaphone.

YACHT GUY
Herbie, my good man! Fantastic seeing you!

Herbie smiles and waves as the yacht sails away.

Herbie reaches inside the tollbooth and pushes the lever. The bridge starts lowering again.

HERBIE
Larry, you get that new hair, and you're gonna get your wife back. And then you're gonna get your whole life back! And that's just the beginning! You don't even know what kind of greatness lies ahead of you after that!

LARRY
Yes! I AM gonna do this! I'm gonna unleash MY hair potential!

The crowd cheers.

HERBIE
Oh Larry, you simply must!

LARRY
I shall!

HERBIE
You mustn't delay!

LARRY
I shan't! I'm gonna get all new hair!

The crowd cheers even louder. Larry gets back into his car.

LARRY
Gosh, Herbie, I am so glad I met you today! I was gonna give up! I was gonna quit on myself!

Larry starts driving away. The crowd starts chanting.

CROWD
Get new hair! Get new hair!

Larry honks as he drives off, and waves goodbye.

LARRY
Thanks, everybody! Herbie, you're the best!

HERBIE
Anytime, Larry. I'm just here to make the world a better place.

Herbie wipes another tear from his face.

CUT TO:

28. Int. Board Game Cafe - Evening

Larry is sitting at a table inside a board game cafe with ALAN and his wife BONNIE.

Alan is completely bald.

They are playing a board game, and the table is filled with bowls of ice cream and empty beer glasses.

Larry is on a phone call, and Alan tries to interrupt.

ALAN
You're going to do WHAT?!?!

LARRY
Sh sh sh... hang on...

ALAN
Larry, we're here to play board games! Get off the phone!

LARRY
(into phone)
Hello? Yes, I'd like to make an appointment for hair surgery. I need all new hair. The full follicle replacement job.

ALAN
WHY?! You have a full head of hair!

LARRY

(into phone)

The earliest. Fastest possible. Tonight? Really? Like tonight tonight?! Yes! Absolutely! I'll see you then!

Larry hangs up the phone.

LARRY

Guys! I got in tonight! Can you believe it?!

Bonnie looks stunned.

BONNIE

Wow. Now that is the free market for you.

ALAN

Larry, what in the world are you doing? Are you drunk?

LARRY

Guys, it finally happened. The family curse. You are officially looking at a bald man. So I gotta do it. I gotta take the plunge.

ALAN

You can't be a bald man if you haven't lost any hair! I'm a bald man!

The waitress walks by, and her tray bangs Alan in the head.

ALAN

Ow!

Alan calls after the waitress.

ALAN

Oh, excuse me, miss? Can I get another beer?

The waitress is gone.

LARRY

See Alan, you don't understand because there's a lot of facts that happened today that you weren't there for. But I AM losing my hair. I saw a professional today, and he assured me that I'm pre-bald.

ALAN

Pre-bald?

Alan looks at his wife.

ALAN

Honey, what is pre-bald?

BONNIE

I think pre-bald means you have hair, right?

LARRY

Yes, yes, technically I HAVE hair. But it's all an illusion. It's not really clamped down. It's not hooked in. It could all go at any moment — the next big wind, maybe even the next big sneeze.

ALAN

So what's the big deal? Go bald! Why would you do the surgery?

LARRY

Are you joking? I could give you a million reasons! But how about the most important reason of all? Lydia! She's gonna take me back if I get all new hair!

BONNIE

The bitch actually said that?

LARRY

First of all, she's not a bitch. And second of all, I can finally see what's going on with her. She won't be able to resist me once I get new hair.

BONNIE

Larry, maybe you should take off that wedding ring and find someone who DOESN'T care about your hair.

LARRY

Well, that person doesn't really exist. Everybody cares. At all times. Except for you, Bonnie. You're a unicorn.

ALAN

She is. She's my little unicorn.

Alan and Bonnie give each other a big kiss on the lips.

A well-haired customer walks by and shouts at Alan.

CUSTOMER

Get a room, baldie!

Alan shouts after the guy.

ALAN

You're just jealous because bald is the best thing that could ever happen to a man!

The waitress walks by, and her tray strikes Alan in the head.

ALAN

Ow!

Alan calls after the waitress.

ALAN

Oh miss? Excuse me? Could I get a —

The waitress is gone.

LARRY

How can you say that bald is a good thing? Have you seen how badly society treats bald men? You can't even get the waitress' attention!

ALAN

There are so many wonderful things about baldness! I mean, have you ever been in a convertible? There's nothing like it when you're bald!

LARRY

No, Alan, my hairstylist just told me today that the whole point of a convertible is to feel the hair whipping in your face.

ALAN

What part of whipping sounds fun to you? And just think about all the other freedoms I have as a bald man!

LARRY

What freedoms?

ALAN

I don't have to waste precious time brushing my hair. I don't have to spend my hard-earned money on haircuts or fancy styling gels! I don't have to worry about the latest hair fashions! Do you remember when mullets went out of style? I mean, there was like a whole year that I didn't even know that. But not my problem anymore. When you're bald, you're free!

LARRY
I don't think so, Alan.

ALAN
What about food? Food tastes so much better without your hair! You wanna know why? Because once you lose your hair, all your senses get heightened!

Alan grabs one of the bowls of ice cream and puts a spoonful of ice cream into his mouth.

ALAN
Mmmmm mmmm mmmm... now THAT is some delicious vanilla ice cream!

LARRY
Alan, that's the lemon sorbet!

The waitress comes by and puts some chicken wings on the table. Alan ducks and covers his head as the waitress walks away.

ALAN
Is she gone?

BONNIE
Yes, sweetie. Would you like me to get you a refill?

ALAN
Yes, please.

Bonnie speaks up.

BONNIE
Miss?

The waitress comes rushing over.

WAITRESS
Yes? How can I help you?

BONNIE

We'll take another beer here.

WAITRESS

Of course.

ALAN

(to Bonnie)

Thank you, baby.

Alan sits up to kiss his wife. The waitress turns around and her tray smacks Alan in the head.

ALAN

Ow!

The waitress is gone.

LARRY

This is what I'm saying! The world is mean to you because you're bald.

ALAN

I don't think the world is mean to me! I love my life! And you can love your life too! It's all about having a positive attitude. I refuse to accept that baldness holds me back in any way.

LARRY

That's great for you, Alan. But you already have it all. I have nothing.

ALAN

You just need to be grateful for all the things you DO have. What do you have that you can be grateful for?

LARRY

Honestly, I can't think of a single thing that I could possibly be grateful for right now.

ALAN

How about your health?

LARRY

Oh yeah, my health. Look, Alan, I PROMISE you that I will be grateful for EVERYTHING as soon as I get my old life back.

ALAN

Larry, you're not getting it. The sooner you're grateful for everything in your life right now, the sooner you won't need your old life back anymore. And you won't need your hair, either.

LARRY

Yeah, I doubt that.

Alan lets out a big sigh.

ALAN

Sweetie, should I tell him?

BONNIE

I think you have to.

LARRY

Tell me what?

ALAN

Larry, we've been best friends since high school, right?

LARRY

Yeah?

ALAN

And we've told each other everything about ourselves, right?

LARRY

Of course! I've told you everything!

ALAN

Well, there's one thing I've never told you. A secret that I've been hiding from you.

LARRY

What?! I can't believe this. What have you been hiding from me?

ALAN

Remember when I got my first job after college and they sent me out of the country for training?

LARRY

Yeah, I remember. They sent you to London.

ALAN

Yeah, that was a lie. They didn't send me anywhere. I took myself to Istanbul.

LARRY

Istanbul! Why?

ALAN

Hair surgery, Larry! I went in for hair surgery!

LARRY

What? But you're bald!

ALAN

I was young. I just found out I was losing my hair. I was terrified of losing everything. I was just like you, Larry. I thought that I could only be happy if I got all new hair. And in my darkest hour, I had to try it. But I was wrong. I went down the wrong path. There are very few things I regret, but this is one of them.

LARRY
I don't get it. What happened?

ALAN
They took my entire scalp! You don't know this about me, but — my entire scalp is made of rubber.

LARRY
You're kidding, right?

ALAN
Stretch it, Larry. Go ahead, stretch it.

Alan leans his head towards Larry.

Larry slowly reaches towards Alan's head. He closes his fingers around the top of Alan's head, and pulls upward.

Alan's head stretches.

LARRY
OH MY GOD! IT'S RUBBER!

ALAN
Not too much. Not too much!

Larry is still stretching Alan's head.

LARRY
OH MY GOD! OH MY GOD!

ALAN
LARRY! STOP STRETCHING MY HEAD!

Larry lets go. Alan's head springs back into place.

LARRY
Sorry! I'm sorry!

ALAN
And there's a metal plate underneath too.

Alan knocks on his head. CLANK CLANK CLANK.

LARRY
I can't believe this!

Larry turns to Bonnie.

LARRY
You've known about this the whole time?

BONNIE
Of course. Originally, he had a choice between pigskin and rubber, but I just couldn't think of my future husband having dead flesh on his scalp.

ALAN
Well, sweetie, it wasn't gonna be rotting. It was gonna be like leather. Like a nice pair of shoes. Cleaned, tanned, polished.

BONNIE
Alan, we talked about this. It was better to go with the synthetic.

LARRY
This is terrible! How could this have happened to you?

ALAN

The surgery went awry. I almost died in there. I was LUCKY that all I lost was my scalp.

LARRY

Oh my God, I'm so sorry. Why didn't you tell me about this sooner?

ALAN

I was humiliated. I didn't want anybody to know. But I'm a stronger man now. And I'm grateful everyday just to be alive. So Larry, please, don't make the same mistake as me. If you really want to beat baldness, you beat it with your attitude.

LARRY

Okay, look, I don't know. I know a guy, and he got the surgery and it's perfect.

ALAN

Well, now you know two guys. And one of them sounds like this.

Alan knocks on his head. CLANK CLANK CLANK.

LARRY

Yeah, but what percentage of men does this really happen to?

ALAN

It's like 40%, Larry!

LARRY

Oh okay, so it's not quite half? It's better than a coin flip?

ALAN

No, Larry, what it means is that for every 10 men that go into surgery, 4 of them come out with a rubber head! Or pigskin!

LARRY

Well, I've got a local guy. I'm not going to Istanbul. I've got American standards on my side. I probably have a 99% chance of success.

ALAN

Larry, please. Don't do anything rash tonight. Just cancel that appointment, go home, and sleep on it. Before you do anything crazy, promise me that you'll think about it.

LARRY

Okay, I'll think about it.

ALAN

You promise?

LARRY

I promise.

CUT TO:

29. Int. Hair Surgeon's Waiting Room - Night

Larry is sitting in the waiting room of a hair surgeon's office. He has a gigantic grin on his face, as he looks around the room excitedly.

There are before & after photos on the walls, and there are photos of people enjoying their new lives with their new hair. There are photos of weddings, picnics, and vacations. All of the photos are signed with words of gratitude for the doctor.

Larry notices a photo of a man driving a convertible. He has long flowing hair with wind whipping through it, and there is a sexy woman sitting next to him. The writing on the photo says, "Thanks, Doc! You're the best!"

Another wall is filled with newspaper articles and magazine cover stories about the hair surgeon.

There is a display case filled with dozens of trophies for hair surgery, including multiple trophies for "Hair Surgeon of the Year". The biggest trophy of all is the "Golden Hair Award". It is shaped like a golden wavy hair follicle and it says, "Lifetime Achievement in Hair Surgery."

A television is playing the hair surgeon's commercial. A handsome man is sitting on the deck of a yacht which is sailing on the ocean. He is playing a ukulele, as two women walk up to him and run their fingers through his beautiful head of hair. The hair surgeon's jingle starts playing: "Snip snip snip, poke poke poke, stitch stitch stitch. It's easy!"

The door to the back room swings open, and a PATIENT with a magnificent head of hair walks out. On his way towards the front door, he speaks to Larry.

PATIENT

This doctor's a genius! He saved my life! That's the only way I can put it! He saved my life!

The patient leaves through the front door, and the HAIR SURGEON walks into the waiting room. He has a full head of hair with black curls that looks like a perm from the 1980's.

HAIR SURGEON

Larry, it's your turn!

LARRY

Oh my God, was that the reporter from Channel 9 News?

HAIR SURGEON

Yep! I did the whole news team!

Larry jumps up and follows the hair surgeon into the back.

CUT TO:

30. Int. Hair Surgeon's Hallway - Night

Larry follows the hair surgeon down a hallway, where the walls are filled with even more photos of men with gorgeous hair. A banner on the wall says, "This Month's Hair Heroes".

LARRY

This place is amazing. Look at all this beautiful hair! I wanna be a hair hero!

Larry notices a photo of a man who resembles Alejandro.

LARRY

Oh my God, that's it! That's what I want! I want long Spanish hair like that!

HAIR SURGEON

That's a great choice, Larry. See that strong flowing mane? It's feminine but it challenges you. It's masculine at the same time.

LARRY

Yes! Just take that and put it on my head!

HAIR SURGEON

I love your enthusiasm, Larry. Positivity always helps the recovery time.

Larry follows the hair surgeon into another room.

CUT TO:

31. Int. Hair Surgeon's Examination Room - Night

They walk into the hair surgeon's examination room, and the hair surgeon closes the door. The walls are filled with certificates and diplomas.

The hair surgeon looks at his clipboard.

HAIR SURGEON
All right, Larry. I understand that you'd like the full follicle replacement.

LARRY
That's right! And I need it done as quickly as possible. It's an emergency.

HAIR SURGEON
Okay, let's see how bad things have gotten. Go ahead and take off your wig.

LARRY
This isn't a wig. This is my real hair. But the follicles are all dead. I need them replaced with fresh, living hair.

HAIR SURGEON
Ah, let me guess. You're going through a mid-life crisis, recently divorced, living in a shed?

LARRY
I'm actually living with my mom. I couldn't afford the shed.

HAIR SURGEON

Okay, Larry. Take off all your clothes and your underwear, and put on this gown. We just need to extract a few hair samples from your donor area — from your upper thigh.

Larry starts undressing.

LARRY

Oh, I thought you were gonna take hairs from my ass!

HAIR SURGEON

Your ass IS your upper thigh, Larry.

The hair surgeon walks over to a computer that has a 3D scanner plugged into it.

HAIR SURGEON

This state-of-the-art 3D scanner is going to analyze your donor hair all the way down to its DNA, and then we're going to upload your results into the government's National Hair Database.

LARRY

Oh! Why are you gonna upload my hair results into some government database?

HAIR SURGEON

In a rare number of cases, some people are not good candidates, so this is how we find out. The government interprets your hair results to make sure your hair is healthy and thriving, and that it will successfully grow in a new location.

LARRY

Okay, now that sounds important!

Larry finishes putting on the assless gown, while the doctor puts on some gloves.

HAIR SURGEON

Oh, before we go too far, do you have any allergies to rubber? Or pigskin? Once you're under, we may need to make decisions in a hurry.

LARRY

Nope. No allergies!

HAIR SURGEON

Well, let's get plucking then! Bend over, Larry.

Larry bends over the examination table.

The doctor walks over with a pair of scissors, and snips some hairs from Larry's ass.

HAIR SURGEON

All right! In just a moment, we'll find out if you're a good candidate.

The doctor walks over to the computer, puts Larry's ass hairs into the 3D scanner, and presses some buttons on the keyboard.

The computer makes a bunch of beeping noises while sophisticated hair analysis charts appear on the screen.

The screen says "Uploading to National Hair Database", and then, "Excellent Candidate".

HAIR SURGEON

Oh Larry, you're an excellent candidate! The government has ranked your ass hair in the 97th percentile!

LARRY

Really? My ass hair is great?

HAIR SURGEON

Your ass hair is wonderful, Larry! I've rarely seen ass hair this springy, this strong, this pliable! You've got practically perfect ass hair.

LARRY

Oh my God, this is amazing! This is the best news I've heard all year! So you can schedule me for surgery?

HAIR SURGEON

If you want, we can squeeze you in for a last-minute surgery tonight.

LARRY

What?! I'm gonna get all new hair tonight? That was my best-case scenario! You're making all my dreams come true, Doc!

HAIR SURGEON

No, Larry. You're not getting new hair tonight.

LARRY

But you just said — the surgery!

HAIR SURGEON

Not hair surgery, Larry. Cryosurgery. We're going to cut out all of your ass hairs and we're going to cryofreeze them in our follicle vault. Then, when you actually start going bald, about 15 years from now, we'll pull them out of cold storage and they'll be ready to go. Fresh as daisies.

LARRY
15 years? No no no! My problems are right now! I need that hair surgery tonight! I need that long flowing Spanish mane of hair tonight!

HAIR SURGEON
You have to understand Larry, I'm not going to work on a perfectly healthy head of hair.

LARRY
But it's not healthy! It's a field of dead wheat! I've already lost my first follicle!

HAIR SURGEON
Calm down, Larry. Nobody goes bald in a day. You've got plenty of time. There's no need to panic.

LARRY
Believe me, your brother would not have sent me here unless this was an emergency!

HAIR SURGEON
MY BROTHER?! My brother put you up to this?! My brother the barber?!

LARRY
He's not a barber, he's a hairstylist.

HAIR SURGEON
Is that what he calls himself? A hairstylist? He's a barber!

LARRY
He's not a barber! He's an artist!

HAIR SURGEON
He's so ungrateful for what I did for him. I gave him the hair surgery.

LARRY

No! He would never put shit hair on his head!

HAIR SURGEON

Oh, is that what he calls it now? Well maybe I should start calling him shithead. Let me assure you, every time you've spoken to him, you've been talking to a shithead.

LARRY

No, don't call him that! He's been a great friend to me!

HAIR SURGEON

How could you be friends with a man like that? He's a fraud. A narcissist. An egomaniac. My brother didn't have the backbone to get through medical school. No, that falls on me, the good but forgotten son. Oh, he's very popular with mom and her friends, because they all want to get their hair done. So I'm the black sheep! But I went to medical school, Larry! Do you know how long that takes? Everyone in society thinks I'm a God. Everyone bows down to me, except my own family! Do you know that my brother stole my ball when I was only 6 years old? Even at 9 years old, he was already a maniac. Now Larry, you listen to me. We can do the cryosurgery, and if your hair is worse in 15 years, you come back and you see me. And next time you see my brother, you tell him that he's nothing but a barber! And I still want my ball back!

LARRY

Doctor! Please! You don't understand what I'm going through! My wife is already sleeping with another man! I'm already training a guy at work! I'm gonna be homeless in a year! Didn't you take some sort of an oath? You have to help me!

HAIR SURGEON

Larry, you're setting off a lot of red flags here.

LARRY

Hey! I can help you too! I'm an I.T. guy. I can set you up with a really nice computer rig. All for free.

HAIR SURGEON

Larry, are you trying to bribe me?

LARRY

No no no! Bribery sounds really illegal. I'm just saying, you scratch my back, I scratch yours.

HAIR SURGEON

That's bribery, Larry.

LARRY

Okay, forget about the rig. I'm just saying that I'm losing everything in my entire life. It's all slipping through my fingers.

Larry drops to his knees and grabs the doctor's legs.

LARRY

I'm afraid. I'm in pain. I just need my life back. Please.

HAIR SURGEON

So, you're saying that your ENTIRE LIFE — EVERYTHING in your ENTIRE LIFE hinges on you getting this hair surgery?

LARRY

YES! YES! Now you understand, Doc!

HAIR SURGEON

Okay, that's EXACTLY the wrong thing to say.

LARRY

What? How could that be —

The doctor presses a button on the keyboard. BEEEEP!

LARRY

Wait! Stop! What did you just do?

HAIR SURGEON

I'm sorry, Larry. I had to lock you out of the system.

Larry jumps to his feet.

LARRY

You what?! What system?

HAIR SURGEON

The National Hair Database. You are now locked out from getting hair surgery anywhere in the entire country.

LARRY

WHAT??! WHY!?!?

HAIR SURGEON

You're a terrible candidate, Larry.

LARRY
You just said that I was an excellent candidate!

HAIR SURGEON
I said your ASS HAIR is an excellent candidate! But YOU, Larry. You are a terrible candidate. You're too emotionally unstable for this procedure.

LARRY
You can't lock me out of getting hair surgery! You know I can just jump on a plane to Istanbul, right? I can get all new hair for 2,000 American dollars!

The doctor hits another button on the keyboard. BEEEEP!

HAIR SURGEON
Not anymore you can't. You're locked out globally.

LARRY
WHAT?! You can do that?!?!

HAIR SURGEON
Oh, I can. And I just did. And you're also locked out from purchasing a gun, too.

LARRY
Okay okay okay, fine fine fine fine, you can freeze my ass hairs for the future. Okay? Let's do that.

HAIR SURGEON
Oh no, Larry. It's too late. Maybe I didn't make myself clear. You're locked out of ALL the procedures. In ALL the places. You'll be lucky if we let you get a head massage.

LARRY

Doc! You can't do this to me! You can't just take my life away with the push of a button!

Larry looks over at the computer and talks calmly while he tiptoes towards it.

LARRY

Okay, listen, listen, listen. I've got an idea. You close your eyes. And I'm just going to click on the button that puts me back into the system again.

HAIR SURGEON

Larry! Get away from that machine!

Larry lunges for the computer and grabs the hard drive.

LARRY

I will hack into this thing! It will say whatever I want it to say!

Larry is frantically trying to rip the cables out of the hard drive, while the doctor is trying to grab the hard drive back from Larry.

HAIR SURGEON

No! Give it back to me! You put that computer down!

Larry and the doctor are fighting over the hard drive, pulling it back and forth.

LARRY

I can see why your brother doesn't talk to you! I'm glad he took your ball! I bet it was his ball all along!

HAIR SURGEON

How dare you! It was my ball! My ball! You don't know my life!

They continue to fight over the hard drive until Larry successfully snatches the entire thing away from the doctor.

LARRY

Ha!

Larry runs towards the door with the hard drive in his hands, when all of a sudden he freezes in place.

We zoom out to reveal that the doctor is holding onto a gigantic clump of Larry's hair, which is still attached to Larry's head.

LARRY

No no no no no, don't pull! Loose follicles — don't pull! We can work this out. Everyone's calm. I'm calm. You're calm. It's just a little misunderstanding. I'm sorry.

HAIR SURGEON

Put that computer down. Or I will yank these hairs out by their roots.

Larry puts down the hard drive.

LARRY

Okay, Doc. Your computer's down. Whatever you say.

HAIR SURGEON

Start walking towards the front door. No sudden moves.

Larry slowly walks towards the door, while the doctor continues to grip onto Larry's hair.

CUT TO:

32. Ext. Strip Mall Parking Lot - Night

The front door of the hair surgeon's office opens, and the hair surgeon pushes Larry out into a strip mall parking lot.

Larry touches all of his hair in a panic, and he talks to his hair.

LARRY
Oh my God! Are all of you guys still okay?
I'm so sorry!

The door slams behind Larry, and we hear the sound of locks bolting.

Larry is wearing nothing but the assless medical gown.

He starts banging on the locked door.

LARRY
Hey, I need my clothes! Please! Doc! You
can't leave me out here like this!

A window opens, and Larry's pants come flying out and land on the ground.

Larry runs over to his pants and bends over to pick them up, while trying to prevent the general public from seeing his butt.

Larry is hopping around on one foot while he attempts to put on his pants, when his underwear comes flying out the window.

Larry pulls off his pants and bends over to pick up his underwear, when one of his shoes comes flying out the window and hits him on the head.

LARRY

Ow! Watch it!

Larry's wallet and keys come flying out the window next. Larry runs over to grab them, and then Larry's phone comes hurling out the window and shatters to pieces when it lands on the ground.

Larry runs over to pick up the remains of his phone, which is now broken and won't turn on.

LARRY

Hey! You broke my phone! You owe me a new one!

Larry throws the broken phone to the ground.

Different pieces of clothing continue to fly out the window, landing in various places all over the sidewalk.

Larry is zig-zagging back and forth to pick up his clothes, all while trying to prevent anybody from seeing his naked butt.

This continues in the background, as we zoom out to reveal a bar which is located right next to the hair surgeon's office.

Standing in front of the bar is HOLLY, a cute woman in her early 30's. She is having an argument with the BOUNCER of the bar.

The bouncer is a tall gigantic stud in his mid-30's. He has rippling muscles and is wearing a tank top. He has a full head of hair with a long mullet.

BOUNCER

But I love you! I just love you so much!

HOLLY

You're an animal! You didn't have to keep hitting him when he was already down!

BOUNCER
But he was naked and you were touching him!

HOLLY
I'm a massage therapist! My job is to touch naked men!

BOUNCER
Okay, but why do YOU have to be naked?

HOLLY
If I could explain that to you, I wouldn't have needed to take all those classes.

BOUNCER
Okay! But I don't understand why you have to shower with them afterwards!

HOLLY
We've been through this already! I'm trying to save water!

BOUNCER
Okay, but what about the sleepovers with your ex? That's cheating!

HOLLY
You can't cheat with an ex! It doesn't count! You've already had sex with that person. There's nothing new there!

BOUNCER
I'm so confused! I don't know! All I know is that I just love you so much!

HOLLY
Shut up and kiss me.

They start kissing each other passionately.

In the background, Larry has gathered all of his belongings into a pile. He tries to hide from people as he puts on his underwear.

The bouncer stops kissing Holly.

BOUNCER

It's just that every time I turn around, you're always kissing some other guy!

HOLLY

No, I'm not! I'm shotgunning them! I'm just blowing weed smoke into their mouth!

BOUNCER

Well I never see any smoke!

HOLLY

Because we always have a perfect, airtight connection!

BOUNCER

Baby, can't you just massage women instead? Then I wouldn't be so crazy!

HOLLY

All my clients are men! Do you want me to go broke just because you're jealous?

BOUNCER

I don't know, I just love you so much! You're so beautiful, I can't take it!

HOLLY

Aw, that's so sweet!

Holly grabs him and starts kissing him again.

Larry scurries towards his car in a partially-dressed state. His pants are on, but the zipper is down and his belt is unbuckled. His shirt is on, but it's open and unbuttoned. His shoes are on, but they're untied and he is holding his socks.

As Larry gets closer to his car, the bouncer notices Larry and stops kissing Holly.

BOUNCER
Oh my God! Who is this? Is this the guy?

HOLLY
Yeah, that's the guy. I'm sleeping with old guys now.

BOUNCER
I don't know who this guy is! Why is some half-naked guy I don't know hanging around you?!

HOLLY
Here we go again.

The bouncer walks over to Larry, grabs him by the shoulders, and pins Larry against his own car.

BOUNCER
Hey! Why aren't you wearing all your clothes? You sleeping with my girl?

LARRY
Oh no no no, you don't understand. I'm not wearing my clothes because I just saw the hair surgeon.

BOUNCER
What?! That doesn't even make any sense! You took off your clothes because of your hair? You know what, I'm gonna beat the shit out of you.

The bouncer makes a fist and pulls back his arm to punch Larry. Larry cringes in fear and closes his eyes, and then Holly walks up.

HOLLY
I can't do this anymore. Tough guy's always gotta beat somebody up.

BOUNCER
But — but I just love you so much!

HOLLY
Awwww, I love you too!

Holly pushes the bouncer up against the driver's door of Larry's car, and she starts making out with him. The bouncer lets go of Larry to embrace Holly.

Larry cautiously opens his eyes.

LARRY
Okay, so I'm gonna go now. If you guys could just move out of the way, please?

The bouncer stops kissing Holly and glares at Larry.

BOUNCER
If you take one step closer to this car, you're gonna wake up in the hospital.

LARRY
Oh yeah, sure. No hurry! I'm not in a rush. I'll just, uh, pop into that bar for a quick drink. So, uh, 10 minutes then?

The bouncer continues to glare at Larry.

LARRY
How about I'll give you 20 minutes. Good. Good plan.

Larry walks up to the door of the bar and looks back. The bouncer is making out with Holly again.

Larry walks into the bar and the door slams shut behind him.

DISSOLVE TO:

33. Int. Mom's Kitchen - Night

There is a real hubbub going on in Larry's mom's kitchen. The room is filled with neighbors and friends who are all urgently making phone calls. There is food everywhere.

We pan by some people and hear snippets of their phone conversations.

FRIEND #1

Please — spread the word that Larry's missing!

FRIEND #2

If you know anyone who's seen Larry, call me back immediately!

FRIEND #3

You gotta get over here. Lucille's shmear is delicious!

He takes a bite of a bagel with shmear.

We see Neighbor Dan, who is also on a phone call. He hangs up his phone and hurries into the next room.

CUT TO:

34. Int. Mom's Living Room - Night

Neighbor Dan rushes into the crowded living room.

NEIGHBOR DAN
Okay, my church has got a search party combing the streets.

Larry's mom is pacing back-and-forth with her phone pressed to her ear. She is muttering into the phone.

LARRY'S MOM
Please pick up, Larry. Please.

Quiet comes over the room as everyone watches Larry's mom.

LARRY'S MOM
Ohhhh! Voicemail again!

The room groans in sympathy. Neighbor Dan speaks up.

NEIGHBOR DAN
Did you call his friends?

LARRY'S MOM
Yes, they're not picking up either!

NEIGHBOR DAN
Okay, let's think carefully about this. Who was the last known person to see Larry alive?

LARRY'S MOM
His hairstylist! That miserable, no-good hairstylist!

She frantically dials her phone and puts it up to her ear. While the phone is ringing, she speaks to the room.

LARRY'S MOM
I'm so sorry, does everybody have enough to eat? There's more shmear in the fridge.

NEIGHBOR DAN
Lucille, we're fine! Stay focused!

The hairstylist picks up the phone. He is in the process of closing up his salon for the night.

HAIRSTYLIST
Hello?

LARRY'S MOM
Hello!? You're gonna talk to me, Mister!

HAIRSTYLIST
I'm sorry, we're closing now. Who is this?

LARRY'S MOM
This is Larry's mother!

HAIRSTYLIST
Yes, and...?

LARRY'S MOM
Larry's gone missing ever since you told him that the curse hit him! Did he tell you where he was going?

HAIRSTYLIST
I don't recall. I don't think much about Larry anymore.

LARRY'S MOM
How dare you! Larry discovered you! Larry was there from the very beginning when

nobody else was sitting in your chair! And now you're too important to talk about whether he's dead in a ditch? Larry made you!

HAIRSTYLIST

Oh, you are mistaken, madam! You've got it twisted, sister! I made Larry! Your boy should've been an egghead by the time he was 30! But I put him on an entire regimen! I kept him relevant! I kept him alive! I'm the one who's been SAVING LARRY'S HAIRLINE all along!

LARRY'S MOM

Larry's not safe out there, thanks to you! The whole world is gonna rip him apart, and you just let him leave your salon?! You couldn't hide him in your attic like a real friend would?

HAIRSTYLIST

Don't come crying to me and telling me this is my fault. Unless you've got a warrant, I'm not responding to any more accusations. I've got hairstylist-client privilege.

The hairstylist hangs up on Larry's mom.

She stares at her phone in shock, and then looks around the room quietly.

NEIGHBOR DAN

Lucille! What did you find out?

LARRY'S MOM

(panicked)

We're gonna need more shmear!

CUT TO:

35. Int. Bar - Night

Inside the bar, Larry walks out of the bathroom. He's fully clothed now.

He looks around the room. The bar is filled with bald men who are sitting alone and drowning their sorrows with alcohol.

There are a few sad-looking Halloween decorations falling off the walls.

Larry walks up to the bar and sits down on a barstool next to a DRUNK BALD GUY.

The BARTENDER has a full head of hair. Larry speaks to him.

LARRY
Excuse me, sir? There's a couple fighting outside. They're blocking my car.

BARTENDER
Oh yeah, that's the bouncer and his girlfriend. They'll burn themselves out in a few hours. What can I get'cha?

LARRY
I don't know if I can have any alcohol. Does alcohol hurt hair? Do you know? I'm trying to keep everything I have.

BARTENDER
Hey man, calm down. I got a shotgun back here.

LARRY

I'm sorry, I just — is there anything back there that's healthy? Do you have any kombucha? Maybe some bone broth? I heard that collagen is good for hair.

BARTENDER

What are you, a hippie? You want some breast milk too?

LARRY

Yes, if you think that would help! You've got breast milk back there?

BARTENDER

No, I don't have breast milk back here. You gonna order something or you gonna get the hell out of my bar?

The drunk bald guy next to Larry speaks up.

DRUNK BALD GUY

Oh, for chrissake, just give the man a beer to hold.

BARTENDER

Beer it is.

The bartender grabs a glass and starts filling it with beer.

LARRY

Okay, well, I guess that worked itself out.

The drunk bald guy looks at Larry.

DRUNK BALD GUY

So what timeline did they give you? 3, 6, 12?

LARRY

Oh my God, you can tell? Is it really that obvious?

DRUNK BALD GUY

It's as plain as the bald on your face. But I got bad news for you.

LARRY

What?

DRUNK BALD GUY

I can tell by those 2 loose hairs in the front that this is gonna happen much faster than any timeline they told you. Those 2 hairs are about to fall out.

LARRY

Please don't stress me out. Stress is a leading cause of baldness.

The bartender plunks down the glass of beer in front of Larry.

DRUNK BALD GUY

Just being real with you. You better get ready. Bald is officially the lowest rung of society. Everything else matters more. Dogs and cats matter more. Somebody raised money for dogs and cats today. Nobody raised money for balds. Nobody cares. You ever see a greeting card that says "I'm sorry your hair fell out"? There's cards for when snot comes out of your nose, and how long is that for? 3 weeks, tops! You're gonna be bald for the rest of your life, and nobody has a shred of sympathy. At least there are a few places left — like this one — where a man doesn't have to slither around to avoid being seen.

The drunk bald guy offers a toast to the bartender, who offers him nothing back but a glare.

BARTENDER
Pipe down, baldilocks.

DRUNK BALD GUY
What, you think I haven't heard that one before?

He turns to Larry.

DRUNK BALD GUY
You believe that crap? Baldilocks? I gotta come out to get insulted?

LARRY
Yeah, that's not fair.

DRUNK BALD GUY
That's not hair?

LARRY
(loudly)
FAIR. That's not FAIR.

DRUNK BALD GUY
Fair? Fuck fair! Fair walked out of my life as soon as it could see its reflection in my forehead.

LARRY
I'm sorry. That sucks.

DRUNK BALD GUY
You'll see for yourself soon enough!

LARRY
Please stop. You're stressing me out.

DRUNK BALD GUY

Well, I see those 2 loose hairs, right there in the front!

LARRY

No, no, you do not see that. You're trying to make things worse than they are.

DRUNK BALD GUY

No no! I see 'em! They're clinging on for dear life! They're hugging, they're crying. They're saying goodbye to their families. This is it! It's over! They're about to go!

The drunk bald guy leans towards Larry and starts blowing on his front hairs.

LARRY

What are you doing? Are you trying to blow my hairs out?!

DRUNK BALD GUY

I know balding when I see it!

Suddenly, the front door of the bar slams open. A BALD STRANGER runs in and starts yelling to the room.

BALD STRANGER

What the hell does "bad candidate" mean?! How the hell can I be a bad candidate?! I need hair!

The bartender yells.

BARTENDER

Hey man, calm down! I got a shotgun back here.

BALD STRANGER

Fuck you! Fuck them! Fuck everybody! I'm going to fucking Istanbul!

The bald stranger runs out of the bar, and the door slams shut behind him.

LARRY

Oh God, that guy is so lucky. He's still got Istanbul. I got locked out of the whole system today. There's gotta be somewhere I can go. Something I can do. There's gotta be some cutting edge technology that can bring my hair back to life again.

DRUNK BALD GUY

Worst advice I ever got was that I could beat this thing. I wasted years trying to beat it. I tried everything. Laser brushes, head massages, shark cartilage infusions, monkey stem cells. Nothing. Sometimes you've just got bad genes. I even tried the surgery.

LARRY

You tried the surgery?

DRUNK BALD GUY

Yep. I'm allergic to rubber. I had to go for the pigskin.

He turns his head around and there's a curly pig tail on the back of his head.

He pulls it to extend the tail. He lets go and it snaps back into a curl again.

LARRY

Oh my God.

DRUNK BALD GUY
Hey, my eyes are down here, buddy.

LARRY
Oh yeah, I'm sorry. I didn't mean to stare.

The front door of the bar slams open again.

Holly storms into the bar. The bouncer is chasing her as she runs up to the bar.

HOLLY
Oh God, I'm so sick of listening to you cry about everything! Why don't you be a real man?! Like any of these guys here!

She points at Larry.

HOLLY
Even this OLD GUY is more of a man than you are!

The bouncer looks at Larry.

BOUNCER
Wait a second! I know you! You're that guy from the parking lot! Son of a bitch! Have you been waiting for me to leave so you can move in on my girl?

LARRY
No, sir! No, sir!

The bouncer grabs Larry by his shirt collar. Larry looks at the bartender.

LARRY
A little help from the shotgun, please?

The bartender shrugs his shoulders.

BOUNCER
(to Holly)
This is the guy you were cheating on me with out in the parking lot!

HOLLY
Yeah, that's what I'm doing. I'm making love to this old guy every night in the backseat of his car.

LARRY
No she's not, sir. No she's not!

HOLLY
And you know why? Because he's a real man! Not like you! He doesn't pine over women like you do!

LARRY
Yes I do, sir! Yes I do!

HOLLY
He's not always chasing me down to see who I'm with or grabbing my phone to see who I'm texting! This is a real man!

Holly grabs Larry and gives him a big smooch on the lips.

BOUNCER
I KNEW IT!
(to Larry)
I'm gonna kick your ass!

The bouncer makes a fist and pulls back his arm to punch Larry. Larry cringes in fear and closes his eyes, and then Holly runs towards the front door.

HOLLY
I'm outta here! I'm leaving you for good!

BOUNCER

No! Don't leave me, baby! Come back here!

Holly runs through the front door and the door slams shut behind her.

The bouncer turns to Larry.

BOUNCER

You wait right here for me. I'm coming back to kick your ass!

The bouncer runs towards the front door and opens it.

BOUNCER

Wait! I love you, baby! We can fix this!

The bouncer runs through the front door and the door slams shut behind him.

The wind from the slammed door blows through the bar. The wind rattles some papers on the corkboard, it blows some napkins off the tables, it chills some people to zip up their jackets, it disturbs some flyers on the bar... and then it ruffles Larry's hair.

IN SLOW MOTION:

We see Larry's eyes looking up at his hair. The bartender's eyes look at Larry's hair. The drunk bald guy's eyes look at Larry's hair.

PLINK! Two hairs fall out of the front of Larry's head.

The opening of "The Blue Danube Waltz" rings out. As the tune plays, the two little hairs drift softly, gracefully down, scissoring past each other, seeming to dance in tandem and in cooperation with each other. It is beautiful.

Larry's eyes follow them all the way down. The bartender's eyes follow them all the way down. The drunk bald guy's eyes follow them all the way down.

The two hairs land in Larry's beer glass.

TIME RETURNS TO NORMAL.

The drunk bald guy cackles with laughter.

DRUNK BALD GUY
Heh heh heh! Welcome to hell, buddy!

Larry starts hyperventilating and mumbling to himself louder and louder.

LARRY
Oh my God, it's happening! It's really happening! I don't have a plan. Oh my God — I don't have a plan! I gotta get outta here! It's zero hour! I gotta get outta here!

Larry stands up and looks frantic.

DRUNK BALD GUY
All right, everybody. Back up. Give the guy some room. A baldening is happening! We've got a live baldening happening, everybody!

Larry is freaking out and running from table to table, yelling at people at each table.

LARRY
I don't know what to do! It's really happening! What am I gonna do? Oh my God, this is it! It's zero hour!

BARTENDER
Hey man, calm down. I got a shotgun back here.

The bartender pulls out the shotgun from behind the bar.

LARRY

No plan! Zero hour! No plan! Zero hour!

BARTENDER

I said calm down! I'm not gonna say it again!

The bartender cocks the shotgun and aims it at Larry.

LARRY

I gotta get outta here!

Larry runs towards the front door and opens it, right as the bartender tilts the shotgun upward and fires a warning shot into the ceiling. KABLAM!

Larry goes running out of the bar.

LARRY

AAAAAAAAAAAAAAAAHH!!

BARTENDER

And don't come back!

Chunks of plaster and debris from the ceiling fall all over the drunk bald guy — onto his head, all over his clothes, and into his beer glass.

He sighs and removes a chunk of plaster from his beer.

DRUNK BALD GUY

Yep. Just another Friday night for a bald man.

He takes a long sip from his glass.

CUT TO:

36. Ext. Downtown Street - Night

Larry is running down the street, screaming like a man on fire.

LARRY
AAAAAAAAAAAAAAAAAHH!!

Larry is running with no idea of where he is or where he is going.

LARRY
Somebody help me! I'm going bald!

Strangers on the street are staring at Larry in alarm.

Larry sees a man with a full head of hair who is working in a fast food drive-thru window.

Larry runs up and pounds his fists on the window. The man shrieks in surprise as Larry shouts.

LARRY
Please help me! I need new hair!

A car in the drive-thru lane blares its horn at Larry.

Larry screams and runs away.

LARRY
AAAAAAAAHH!

Larry runs up to an apartment building and starts buzzing all the buzzers on the front door.

LARRY
Somebody help! Zero hour! Hair! Wife! Life!

A voice comes from the speaker box:

VOICE (O.S.)

Hello? Who is this? I'm calling the cops on you!

Larry sees a man riding a bike and starts chasing him.

LARRY

Please help me! I just want my life back!

The bicyclist is terrified and rides off quickly.

Larry is running, sweating, and completely out of breath.

Just then, he spots an all-night pharmacy. He goes running towards the pharmacy doors.

CUT TO:

37. Ext. Pharmacy - Night

Larry slams into the glass front doors of the pharmacy, nearly collapsing. He can't get the door open. He bangs on the door. He pushes on it, but it won't open. He keeps banging and pushing. He sees the PHARMACIST inside, who is standing behind the front counter and waving Larry to come inside.

LARRY

I don't know what to do! I'm pushing! Please help me! Open up!

The pharmacist makes a pulling hand motion, and shouts loudly through the glass.

PHARMACIST

PULL on the door! PULL!

Larry pulls the door open and runs inside.

CUT TO:

38. Int. Pharmacy - Night

Larry rushes inside, scanning aisles in a frenzy. He runs down an aisle, frantically grabbing products off the shelves and filling up his arms. He is mumbling incoherently.

The PHARMACIST, a bald man in his mid 30's, is wearing a white lab coat with a black t-shirt underneath that says "FUCK YOU" in big white letters. He is reading a porn magazine. The cover shows a naked woman going down on a Tibetan monk while the monk throws cash in the air.

Larry approaches the front counter, carrying an immense number of bottles, jars, boxes, and tubes. He leans forward and drops everything on the counter.

LARRY
I've got a plan... I've got a plan...

PHARMACIST
Whoa! What the hell is this? What sort of plan is this?

LARRY
New hair!

PHARMACIST
This ain't no plan! You just gonna buy everything? You just gonna put all this shit on your head? Jesus — this one's for hemorrhoids!

LARRY
I just want my life back!

PHARMACIST

Look, shut the fuck up a second.

The pharmacist slaps Larry.

LARRY

Ow!

PHARMACIST

When I took my pharmacist's oath, I swore to help guys like you. And if you think for a second I'm gonna let you fuck up my oath, then you're a selfish asshole.

LARRY

I'm sorry. But they locked me out of the system! They won't let me do the surgery! I even have perfect ass hairs!

PHARMACIST

Do me a favor. Shut the fuck up a second. I know the fix and it's not sticking some ass hairs through your head. You've heard of priscillas, right?

LARRY

Priscillas? I think so... it's one of these cocktails, right?

Larry starts rifling through the mess of products on the counter.

The Pharmacist picks up a trash can, and with one big swipe of his arm, he pushes all the products into the trash.

PHARMACIST

Guy, if those things were gonna work, you'd be taking them by now. You want to prevent your head from looking like a cue ball? You take only one thing. Priscillas.

LARRY

Priscillas.

PHARMACIST

Yeah, like the Greek goddess. You put it on your noggin, and I guaran-fuckin-tee you, new hair. I take priscillas every day!

LARRY

But... you're bald.

PHARMACIST

Nah nah nah, I WAS bald. But look now.

The pharmacist bends forward and pulls Larry's face into his head.

PHARMACIST

Little baby hairs. Firmly rooted. Sprouting anew.

He lifts his head back up.

PHARMACIST

My hair is in MUCH better shape than your hair.

LARRY

How come I've never heard of priscillas before?

PHARMACIST

You wanna come back in a year when you've heard of it?

LARRY

No!

PHARMACIST

Then shut the fuck up a second. I got my hair back, I got my confidence back, I even got a new girlfriend.

The pharmacist turns around the porn magazine that he's looking at, and shows a naked woman to Larry.

LARRY

That's your girlfriend?

PHARMACIST

Sure, why not. Whoa! Guy! You're shedding hairs all over my counter here!

The pharmacist swipes several of Larry's hairs off the counter towards Larry. They all fall onto the floor at Larry's feet.

LARRY

Oh my God! It's happening even faster than I thought!

PHARMACIST

Guy! Will you stop worrying? You're gonna have so much new hair! Just shut the fuck up a second and come with me.

The pharmacist walks towards the back door of the pharmacy. Larry follows him.

CUT TO:

39. Ext. Back Alley Behind Pharmacy - Night

A heavy metal door scrapes against the concrete as it opens. The pharmacist and Larry emerge. Larry follows the pharmacist towards a rundown brown van.

LARRY
Wait, which goddess was priscillas? I don't think I've heard of her.

PHARMACIST
The fat yellow one. Listen guy, don't get distracted now. It's game time. You want to win? You want to beat this thing?

LARRY
Oh God, yes. Just yesterday, I was a well-haired man.

PHARMACIST
Hey, that's a great story, thanks for sharing. Now shut the fuck up a second. What you're trying to do is basically the impossible. You're trying to make something grow in a wasteland. And that's what priscillas does. Priscillas does the impossible. It's magic in a bottle.

The pharmacist opens the back of the van to reveal a large wooden pallet that is holding a dozen mason jars, all glowing green from some mysterious green bubbling goop inside of them. There is smoke emanating from the jars.

LARRY
This stuff can really grow hair?

PHARMACIST
Ho ho ho, growing hair is NOT the problem.

LARRY
Oh, so there IS a problem?

PHARMACIST
Look guy, as long as you can't get pregnant, you don't have a goddamn thing to worry about.

LARRY
So there's no side effects then?

PHARMACIST
No, none, zero. All that shit was bullshit. It was just some shitty grandmothers complaining about a little smell.

LARRY
I just don't want to wake up and find out I caused some genetic damage or something.

PHARMACIST
Hey guy, this shit is GUARANTEED to alter you genetically! If your genes were any fuckin' good, you wouldn't be in this situation to begin with!

LARRY
That's true! My genes are terrible! I have a family curse!

PHARMACIST
Look, your head already knows how to grow hair. Priscillas just reprograms your DNA to do it again.

LARRY

This sounds incredible. Where did you get this stuff?

PHARMACIST

Don't worry about it. I got a guy. Look, do you want new hair or do you want to dicker all night?

LARRY

No no no... I definitely want new hair!

The pharmacist grabs the pallet out of the van and hands it to Larry. Larry grunts from the weight.

Some of the green goop spills onto the pharmacist's hand. He quickly wipes it off with his white lab coat.

PHARMACIST

Now guy, there's one thing you have to know. Just use one drop per day.

He points to an eyedropper that's attached to the pallet.

LARRY

Okay, got it.

PHARMACIST

No seriously, guy. I mean it. JUST. ONE. DROP.

LARRY

Yeah, I got it. One drop per day.

PHARMACIST

One drop's the maximum. Not two drops because you get some fancy idea in your head... no, one drop a day max.

LARRY
Okay, okay! How do I get more of this when I run out?

PHARMACIST
You're not gonna need any more, guy! One drop per day! And besides, there is no more. This is the VERY LAST BATCH. My guy had to shut down operations. But you've got enough priscillas to pass down to your children for generations! Now where's your wallet?

LARRY
In my back pocket?

The pharmacist grabs the wallet out of Larry's back pocket, opens it up, and grabs the cash.

PHARMACIST
This is all you got? 400 bucks?

LARRY
I can give you a credit card.

PHARMACIST
Guy! This is a cash-only product!

He stuffs the cash into his jeans and returns the wallet to Larry's pocket.

PHARMACIST
Wow, this really is your lucky day. Sold for only 400 bucks.

LARRY
That's a great deal for new hair! I can't thank you enough!

PHARMACIST

Get out of here, you silly kid. Go enjoy your hair!

Larry gleefully walks away with the pallet.

The pharmacist looks down at his hand and his lab coat, both of which have already sprouted thick patches of hair from where the priscillas touched.

PHARMACIST

Ah, shit.

He grabs an electric razor out of the back of his van and starts shaving his hand.

CUT TO:

40. Ext. Pharmacy - Night

In front of the pharmacy, a government van pulls up. The side of the van reads “Federal Unit for Cosmic Knowledge and Extraterrestrial Research”.

A bunch of government agents, armed with weapons and wearing bulletproof vests, jump out of the van and storm through the front door of the pharmacy.

CUT TO:

41. Int. Pharmacy - Night

Inside the pharmacy, the government agents are running up and down the aisles.

The CHIEF AGENT enters the pharmacy wearing a suit and tie. He is mostly bald, except for a sweaty combover of his few remaining hairs.

CHIEF AGENT
Boys, I want you to rip this place apart! I want that priscillas in my hands in 3 minutes!

The ASSISTANT AGENT, a young man with a full head of hair, runs up to the chief.

ASSISTANT AGENT
Sir, we're not allowed to ransack anymore. We went through sensitivity training.

CHIEF AGENT
Oh, Jesus Christ. I miss the good ol' days.

The pharmacist walks in from the back door of the pharmacy.

He is smiling and whistling until he notices the team of government agents.

PHARMACIST
Whoa! What the hell is going on in here?

A government agent runs up to the pharmacist and points his gun at him. The pharmacist quickly raises his hands.

PHARMACIST
Whoa whoa whoa!

CHIEF AGENT
Surround him, boys!

ASSISTANT AGENT
New rules, sir. We can only point one gun at a time. Sensitivity.

CHIEF AGENT
Jesus Christ.

The chief walks up to the pharmacist and handcuffs him.

CHIEF AGENT
All right, Kowalski. You're under arrest. Now tell us what we want to know. Where's the priscillas?

The pharmacist shrugs his shoulders.

PHARMACIST
I don't know.

The assistant pulls the chief aside.

ASSISTANT AGENT
He says he doesn't know, sir.

CHIEF AGENT
I heard what he said! So work him! Get it out of him!

ASSISTANT AGENT
Well, it seems unlikely that he'd answer the question differently if I did the asking, sir.

CHIEF AGENT
Are you kidding me? I got a man to admit to crimes he'd never even heard of before, all

because I grilled him for four hours! Now get in there!

ASSISTANT AGENT
Sir, shouldn't we wait for his attorney to get here?

CHIEF AGENT
If you ever say that to me again, I'm going to strangle you.

The chief turns to the pharmacist.

CHIEF AGENT
All right, Kowalski. Stop playing games. We don't even want you. We just want the substance back in the government lab where it belongs. If you cooperate with us, I'll go easy on you. You'll be a free man by morning. But if you lie to us, it could be life in prison.

PHARMACIST
Oh, please. You've got nothing on me. You've got no evidence. I got rid of all the surveillance cameras months ago. I don't need to tell you anything!

A government agent runs in the front door, holding a drone.

GOVERNMENT AGENT
We got the drone footage, sir! He sold the priscillas to a white guy, 5'11", brown hair, blue eyes!

PHARMACIST
Yeah yeah yeah! What do you guys want to know? I sold it to a white guy! 5'11", brown hair, blue eyes!

CHIEF AGENT
You sold it? For what purpose?

PHARMACIST
Growing hair?

CHIEF AGENT
Oh, Jesus Christ! Growing hair is a SIDE EFFECT! We don't even know if that stuff's really hair! Priscillas is alien technology! It's dangerous! It's some kind of alien artificial intelligence! We need it back in our lab immediately. It's like a ticking time bomb!

PHARMACIST
What?! Nobody ever told me! How was I supposed to know?

CHIEF AGENT
You're not supposed to know any of this! That's why it was locked up in Area 51! Now who'd you sell the priscillas to? Tell us who he is!

PHARMACIST
I don't know! I don't know his name! I don't know how to find him!

CHIEF AGENT
Then you better say hello to life in prison, Kowalski. Let's go!

The chief starts pulling the handcuffed pharmacist towards the front door, passing by the counter.

PHARMACIST
Wait wait wait! His hairs! They're on the floor right over there!

The pharmacist points his head towards the floor in front of the counter.

CHIEF AGENT

Everybody freeze!

The chief gets down on his hands and knees, and picks up one hair from the ground. The hair gleams in the light.

CHIEF AGENT

Gotcha!

He stands up.

CHIEF AGENT

Boys, get me a mobile hair analyzer! Pronto! We need to run this through the National Hair Database!

The assistant pulls out an electronic device from his vest. The device looks like an oversized smartphone.

ASSISTANT AGENT

Um, we're not supposed to use this without a warrant, sir.

CHIEF AGENT

I'll warrant your ass right back to basic training! Now give me that!

The chief grabs the electronic device and sticks the hair into a small hole on the side. The device starts beeping, and then it makes a loud buzzing sound.

CHIEF AGENT

Oh, Jesus Christ! Our person of interest. His name's Larry. He got red-flagged in the system.

ASSISTANT AGENT
He got completely locked out? What for?

CHIEF AGENT
Emotional instability! Oh no no no, priscillas can't be around anyone who's emotionally unstable. It can't be around ANY unstable conditions. It can't be too hot, it can't be too cold, it can't be too loud, it can't be too bright. Everything has to be just right! Priscillas needs to be under a perfectly controlled climate of 72 degrees with classical music playing at all times! It can't be shaken up. It can't be stirred. It needs to be completely still. And it can't be around any negative emotions! It must be whispered to in a positive voice. If you get it riled up, it'll become sentient. It'll start to wake up and realize it's alive. Top government minds have been studying this thing for 6 years, and we hardly know more now than we knew then! All we try to do is keep it asleep!

CUT TO:

42. Ext. Downtown Street - Night

Larry is walking happily down the street, humming to himself.

He is carrying the pallet of mason jars, which are clinking as he walks. Their contents are glowing green and bubbling.

CUT TO:

43. Ext. Strip Mall Parking Lot - Night

Larry approaches his parked car in the strip mall parking lot.

We follow Larry to the back of his car as he opens the trunk.

In the background, we hear Holly and the bouncer.

BOUNCER (O.S.)
I just love you so much! My life would be over without you!

HOLLY (O.S.)
Then say you're sorry!

Larry looks around to find the voices, but he doesn't see anyone. He places the pallet of priscillas into the trunk.

BOUNCER (O.S.)
I'm sorry!

HOLLY (O.S.)
This is the last time I forgive you! Now kiss me, you animal!

Larry closes his trunk, which reveals — to Larry's horror — that Holly and the bouncer are sitting on the hood of his car, making out with each other. Holly is holding a bottle of whiskey.

Larry walks towards the front of the car.

LARRY
Wow, guys, it's so great to see you like this. I'm so happy for you. I just need to get out of here now.

The bouncer stops kissing Holly and looks at Larry.

BOUNCER
Oh my God, man! Can't you see that my whole life is at stake here? What the hell do you want, man?

Larry is frozen in fear.

LARRY
I... just want to go home... put some stuff on my head... sprout some new hair...

The bouncer jumps off the hood and approaches Larry.

BOUNCER
Wait a minute! You're that guy from before! You're the guy who's doing my girl!

HOLLY
Seriously? Again? I can't do this anymore.

Larry starts to back away.

LARRY
Oh, no no no. I don't do anyone. I don't even do myself. I'll just leave you two alone...

Larry turns to run, but the bouncer forcefully grabs Larry by his hair.

LARRY
No, no, no! Loose hairs, loose hairs! Could you please just put me in a chokehold?

BOUNCER
I can't believe tonight's the night I have to kill a guy.

The bouncer lifts Larry up by his hair.

We hear a small ripping sound from Larry's head as Larry's feet leave the ground.

HOLLY

Go ahead, tough guy. I'd love to see you kill the old man.

LARRY

Not helping!

Larry's feet are dangling in the air while the ripping sound grows louder.

The bouncer grabs a heavy flashlight out of his pocket.

BOUNCER

I really didn't want to do this to you, but you ruined my life!

He coils his arm back, ready to strike Larry with the flashlight, when Holly appears behind him, holding the whiskey bottle high in the air.

HOLLY

We're officially broken up!

Holly crashes the whiskey bottle over the bouncer's head and he crumples to the ground.

As he crumples, we hear the loudest ripping sound of all. A gigantic tuft of hair is torn out of Larry's head.

LARRY

AAAAAAAAHHHHHHHHHHHH!!!

Larry is now visibly down to 80% of his hair. 20% of his hair is now gone. It's in the hand of the bouncer.

Larry's head is bleeding. He touches his head, then looks down and sees the body of the bouncer.

LARRY

Oh my God, is he dead?

HOLLY

No, he'll be up in a second and he's gonna kill both of us! Give me your keys, we gotta move NOW!

Larry is bewildered and in pain, holding his head, staring at the body. He pulls his keys out of his pocket.

Holly grabs the keys, gets in the driver's seat, and starts the car.

We hear the Blue Diamond meditation flute from inside the car.

BLUE DIAMOND (V.O.)

Peace and joy are in the air. Deeply breathe it in.

Larry takes a few steps towards the car, then stops and runs back to snatch his hair out of the bouncer's hand. The bouncer begins stirring.

Holly starts pulling the car away.

LARRY

Wait! My car!

Larry runs to the car, flings open the back door, and manages to jump into the back seat of the car, right as Holly speeds off.

CUT TO:

44. Int./Ext. Larry's Car - Night

Holly is driving like a lunatic down the road.

HOLLY
Woohoo! I am FREE!

She swerves onto the sidewalk.

LARRY
Oh my God! Road! ROAD!

Holly swerves back onto the road again.

HOLLY
You were so courageous back there! You saved me from my boyfriend! My EX-BOYFRIEND now! Hahaha!

LARRY
What are you talking about? You were the one who saved me!

HOLLY
Awwww, we saved each other! It was destiny! Tell me your name!

LARRY
I'm Larry!

HOLLY
Nice to meet you! I'm Holly!

She turns around to shake his hand. The car swerves into oncoming traffic as cars blare their horns and screech their brakes.

LARRY

No no no, turn around! Keep your hands on the wheel!

HOLLY

Oh, please, Larry! I can drive these streets with my eyes closed. Watch!

LARRY

No no no! I believe you!

She closes her eyes. The car almost hits a pole, when Larry frantically lunges forward from the backseat and grabs the wheel. Larry swerves the car back onto the road.

Holly opens her eyes and starts steering again.

HOLLY

Oh, Larry! I feel amazing! Where are we going? The Day of the Dead Festival?

LARRY

No! You need to take me to the hospital!

HOLLY

Hospital? Why?

LARRY

To get these hairs sewn back onto my head!

HOLLY

You look so hot when your head is bleeding. I love that on a guy.

LARRY

Maybe we should stop for ice first. I think I need to keep these on ice.

HOLLY

Pshhhaww. You don't need those.

She rolls down the window, grabs the clump of hairs from Larry's hand, and throws them out.

LARRY
No no no no no! What did you just do?!

HOLLY
Relax! I've got a guy who can fix you right up! He's my neighbor!

She lets go of the steering wheel and starts texting on her phone with both hands.

LARRY
The wheel!

Larry lunges forward and grabs the steering wheel again.

HOLLY
Shhhh! I'm texting my neighbor for you!

LARRY
Can't you call him instead?!

Holly starts giggling, and grabs the wheel again.

HOLLY
Oh, Larry! You are so funny! I like you! Tell me about your past. What kind of a kid were you?

LARRY
Look, why don't you pull over so I can drive?

She turns around to look at Larry.

HOLLY
You didn't answer my question!

Holly hits a curb and the tire rim starts sparking.

HOLLY

What the hell was that?

She sticks her head out the window.

LARRY

Please! Pull over!

HOLLY

Not until you tell me about your childhood!

LARRY

I — I — I won the spelling bee in 6th grade!

Holly squeals in delight, and looks at Larry.

HOLLY

Whaaaaat! I was the worst in spelling! Why don't they spell "cough" with an "f"?

Suddenly, a police siren and flashing lights emerge behind them.

HOLLY

Oh, these pigs always ruin the mood.

LARRY

Oh no, this is not good. This is not part of the plan.

HOLLY

Plan. Now that's a word I don't hear much!

Holly pulls over, lights up a joint, and starts smoking it.

LARRY

What are you doing?! Put that out! Oh my God, I'm going to jail.

HOLLY

Shhhh. They can smell fear.

LARRY
Can they smell weed?!

The ominous sound of footsteps approaches the car.

HOLLY
Be calm.

The face of a white POLICEMAN lowers into the window. He has a full head of neatly combed hair.

POLICEMAN
We about to give birth tonight? Or we just out of our minds on meth?

Holly starts shrieking.

HOLLY
Oh my God! Ahhhhhhhhhhhh!

Larry starts shrieking.

LARRY
Ahhhhhhhhhhhh!

HOLLY
Ahhhhhhhhhhhh! I can't believe it! I know this pig!

POLICEMAN
Hey! Holly! How you doing, girl?

Holly grabs the policeman and gives him a big french kiss. Larry is awestruck.

HOLLY
Oh, shit! When did you get out of prison?

POLICEMAN

I just got out. It was a life-changing experience. Did you know that all races should be treated equally?

HOLLY

Duh! You should have asked me!

POLICEMAN

Well, I didn't know! Jesus, you smell like you just came back from Jamaica. Who's this?

HOLLY

Oh, this is my Larry. Isn't he adorable?

LARRY

Good evening, officer.

POLICEMAN

Oh man, does he know what's gonna happen if you two get caught together?

HOLLY

Not anymore. I dumped the bastard tonight!

POLICEMAN

Well! In that case...

The policeman grabs Holly and gives her a big french kiss.

HOLLY

Mmm, mmm... I love me some spice.

POLICEMAN

Is there any way I could expect you to have your license on you?

HOLLY

Nooo! You know me!

The policeman turns to Larry.

POLICEMAN
How about you? You got one?

LARRY
Yes, but you can't give me a ticket, right? I mean, I wasn't driving, right?

POLICEMAN
Well, I'm assuming it's your car, so unless you want me to impound it...

LARRY
No, that's okay, officer. Here's my license! I'll take the ticket, please! Thank you very much!

Larry hands his license to the policeman. The policeman gives Holly a disapproving look.

POLICEMAN
No way is this guy your type.

HOLLY
My NEW type!

The policeman inserts Larry's license into a mobile printer, and a ticket comes printing out of it.

POLICEMAN
Okay, a ticket for you...

He hands the ticket to Larry.

POLICEMAN
And a warning for you.

He takes his finger and gently boops Holly on the nose.

POLICEMAN
Boop! Now get home and get this car off the road. I don't want to have to give you a second warning.

The policeman turns and walks back to his vehicle.

HOLLY
Love ya, pig! Oink oink!

Holly starts driving again.

LARRY
Oh God, I think my heart stopped.

HOLLY
Relax Larry! Everyone knows that stress is bad for hair!

Larry runs his hand through his hair. When he looks at his fingers, they are full of another tuft of bloody hair. He sags in his seat, then looks up.

LARRY
Road. Road! ROAD!

DISSOLVE TO:

45. Ext. Apartment Courtyard - Night

Larry's car is parked in front of the courtyard of an apartment building.

Larry and Holly get out of the car, and they walk through the courtyard. There are stairs leading up, but Holly stops at a door on the ground floor.

She knocks on the door. We hear the sound of a dog yapping.

HOLLY

Here we are! This guy's the best acupuncturist, probably in the world. He's the grandmaster.

LARRY

Acupuncture? Oh, no no no, I need way more than that. A few needles in my head is not gonna fix this. I need serious help.

She punches Larry in the gut.

LARRY

Ow!

HOLLY

Do NOT disrespect the grandmaster! He got me to quit smoking. Twice!

She knocks on the door again.

We hear feet shuffling behind the door, then the sound of several locks opening.

An ancient Asian man opens the door, glasses slightly askew. He is completely bald, and he is holding a little dog.

ACUPUNCTURIST
Huh? Whuh?

Larry goes to pet the dog.

LARRY
Hi little guy!

The dog snaps at Larry. RAWR! Larry yanks his hand back.

LARRY
My mistake!

HOLLY
Hey grandmaster! Did I wake you?

ACUPUNCTURIST
Ya?

HOLLY
You didn't get my texts?

ACUPUNCTURIST
No! Wassamata?

HOLLY
It's an emergency! This is my Larry. He's losing his hair. I told him you could help.

ACUPUNCTURIST
Lose a hair? Ya, ya, I make you head full a hair. No problem. Easy fix.

Larry whispers to Holly.

LARRY
But... he's bald.

She punches Larry in the gut.

LARRY

Ow!

ACUPUNCTURIST

You dump boyfriend for Larry?

HOLLY

That's right! I broke up with him tonight! Larry's my new boyfriend!

She wraps her arms around Larry and kisses him on the cheek.

LARRY

But we just met each other tonight.

HOLLY

I know, right?! It's amazing how fast this is happening!

The acupuncturist's face lights up.

ACUPUNCTURIST

Old boyfriend gone?

HOLLY

Yep! Bye bye!

ACUPUNCTURIST

Bye bye? Really gone?

HOLLY

Really gone!

The acupuncturist turns to Larry.

ACUPUNCTURIST

Really really gone?

LARRY

Yeah, I saw the breakup. It looked pretty bad.

ACUPUNCTURIST

It looked bad? I so happy! Larry, when you get angry, you beat up old man?

LARRY

No! I would never beat up an old man!

ACUPUNCTURIST

Ohhh! Welcome to family, Larry!

He gives Holly and Larry a big group hug, and then he starts jumping for joy.

ACUPUNCTURIST

Happy happy day! I can't believe it!

He throws the dog in the air like a baby and then catches it.

ACUPUNCTURIST

I don't have to be afraid for my life anymore?

HOLLY

Nope!

ACUPUNCTURIST

Oh, happy happy!

The acupuncturist throws the dog in the air towards Holly.

Holly catches the dog. The dog licks Holly. She giggles and throws the dog to Larry.

Larry catches the dog, and the dog starts barking and snarling at Larry. RAH RAH RAH! GRRRRRRRRR!

LARRY

Whoa! Whoa!

Larry immediately throws the dog to the acupuncturist. He catches the dog and continues jumping for joy.

ACUPUNCTURIST

Happy happy family! Larry, I give you best acupuncture in whole lifetime! I use biggest fattest needles on you!

LARRY

Oh no, that's okay. Small needles are fine.

ACUPUNCTURIST

Give me 5 minutes! I text you when I'm ready. So happy!

HOLLY

Thank you, grandmaster!

The acupuncturist closes the door.

HOLLY

Come on, Larry! Let me show you my place!

Holly goes running up the stairs, and Larry follows.

She unlocks the door to her apartment and walks inside.

CUT TO:

46. Int. Holly's Apartment - Night

Larry follows Holly into her apartment and closes the door behind him.

Immediately, Holly pushes Larry up against the door and starts kissing him.

HOLLY
Oh Larry, what an incredible night! You freed me! I think I love you!

She grabs his hand and puts it on her breast.

HOLLY
Touch me, Larry! Kiss me! I'm yours now! You won me!

Larry makes out with her for a few moments, and then pulls his hand away and breaks away from the kisses.

LARRY
Oh God, no, I'm so sorry. I can't do this. I'm in love with someone else.

He holds up his hand to show Holly his wedding ring.

HOLLY
Noooo! You can't be married! You're the last good man!

Holly storms over to her couch and plops down on it.

HOLLY
I don't care who she is! She doesn't love you like I love you!

LARRY

Ha, you could be right about that. She divorced me 6 months ago.

HOLLY

Wait, what? You mean you're actually single?

LARRY

Technically, I'm single. But emotionally, I'm still married. I'm holding out hope that we're gonna get back together. Especially once I get the hair that she loves.

HOLLY

Aw, you poor thing. Come here. Haven't people told you to move on?

Larry walks over to the couch and sits next to Holly.

LARRY

Yeah, yeah. People have been telling me to move on.

HOLLY

Well, this is how you move on! We're moving on together! I mean, this is really destiny! What are the chances that I would break up with my boyfriend on the very same night that you're looking to move on?

LARRY

I see what you're saying, but I wasn't really looking to move on...

HOLLY

Oh my God, you are loyal as fuck. That is so hot. It's so hard to find a loyal man these days. Tell me, Larry, what's your zodiac sign?

LARRY

Aries?

HOLLY

I'm a Leo! We're twin flames! We're perfect for each other! What sign was your wife?

LARRY

Gemini?

HOLLY

Ohhhhh, Larry! You never should've been married to that person! You could've asked me. I would've told you!

Holly grabs a joint from the coffee table.

HOLLY

You wanna smoke some weed? I make all my best decisions stoned.

LARRY

Oh God, I think one of the reasons my wife divorced me was because I wouldn't smoke weed with her.

HOLLY

So you don't want any?

LARRY

Oh, no! I'm not making that mistake again! This is new Larry! Give me some weed!

HOLLY

Yay! I'll shotgun you. I'm gonna blow the smoke into your mouth, and you just relax and breathe in, okay?

LARRY

Okay.

She lights the joint, inhales a big puff, presses her lips up to Larry's lips, and blows.

Larry sucks it in, and starts coughing.

LARRY

Holy cow, this is strong!

She gives Larry little kisses on his face.

HOLLY

Oh, Larry. I wanna know everything about you. What's your spirit animal? How would you most like to die? What's your favorite food? Is it pizza? Tell me it's pizza because mine is pizza!

LARRY

Yeah yeah, I love pizza!

HOLLY

Oh my God! What's your favorite topping?

LARRY

Sausage?

HOLLY

Ahhhhhh! I love sausage! Oh my God, my parents are going to be so happy to meet you! I always told them I would date a doctor!

LARRY

I'm not a doctor.

HOLLY

You're not? What do you do?

LARRY

I'm an I.T. guy.

HOLLY

Ah, close enough! Same thing.

Larry touches the wounds on his head.

HOLLY

Let me take a look at your head. You know, it doesn't really look that bad. But let me get you something to put on that.

She walks into the kitchen, grabs a paper towel, and pours some whiskey on it.

HOLLY

Here, this'll make it better.

She comes back and puts the paper towel on Larry's head.

LARRY

Ahhhh... that stings!

She removes the paper towel and kisses him on the forehead. Larry smiles.

LARRY

That does feel a little better. You know, before, whenever I would get hurt, my wife would get disgusted and just tell me to suck it up.

HOLLY

Well, she wasn't your destiny! Duh!

LARRY

Maybe you're right. Maybe it is time for me to move on. I really do like you, even though I hardly know you. You're beautiful, you've got such positive energy, and you're full of surprises — in a good way.

HOLLY

And you're so normal! I feel so safe around you. I don't normally date old guys, but everything has changed now!

She leans in and kisses Larry on the lips. He looks happy.

LARRY

Let me ask you a question.

HOLLY

Ask me anything you want!

LARRY

I have a timeshare in Hawaii.

HOLLY

Hawaii?! Ahhhhhh!! Oh my God!! I've never been! Is it wonderful?

LARRY

Well, I don't know how you feel about paradise, but I think it's great.

HOLLY

I love paradise! I've always wanted to go there!

LARRY

Well, let's say that we went there every year for regular vacations.

HOLLY

Ahhhhhhhh!! I'd call that a tradition! We'd have a Hawaii tradition! How great would that be!!

LARRY

See?! Thank you! That's exactly how I feel about it!

HOLLY

Can we do the same activities every year? I hate doing things just once!

LARRY

It's like you're reading my mind.

HOLLY

That's what I'm telling you, Larry! It's destiny for us to be together!

Holly embraces Larry and gives him another big kiss on the lips.

Her phone buzzes, and she looks down at it.

HOLLY

Oh, he's ready for you.

LARRY

You know, I don't really need acupuncture tonight. We can just keep talking and get to know each other better.

HOLLY

No, Larry. You go get your hair fixed. And I'll be right here waiting for you. We've got the rest of our lives to get to know each other.

CUT TO:

47. Ext. Apartment Courtyard - Night

Larry knocks on the acupuncturist's door. A moment later, the door opens and the acupuncturist greets Larry.

ACUPUNCTURIST

Ahhh, Larry! Soooo happy! Come in! Come in!

Larry walks in.

CUT TO:

48. Int. Acupuncturist's Apartment - Night

The apartment is filled with Asian decorations and artwork. There is an acupuncture table in the middle of the room.

The acupuncturist pinches Larry's cheek.

ACUPUNCTURIST
New boyfriend perfect! I give you family rate, which is free!

LARRY
Thank you, grandmaster, but I'm not really sure if acupuncture is strong enough for my hair.

ACUPUNCTURIST
Nonsense! Acupuncture turn you right around! Acupuncture fix whole life!

The dog runs up to Larry, starts snarling, and begins tearing at Larry's pants. GRRRRRRRRR!

LARRY
Whoa, whoa! Calm down, buddy!

ACUPUNCTURIST
Awww, he like you.

The acupuncturist grabs the dog and throws him like a rag doll onto a dresser next to the acupuncture table.

ACUPUNCTURIST
Now lie down on table. Let me feel your pulse.

Larry lies down on the table. The acupuncturist puts two fingers on Larry's wrist.

ACUPUNCTURIST

Ah, liver strong. Lungs strong. Kidneys in very good shape! Oh, weak hair. Very weak hair.

LARRY

Yes! I have all loose hair follicles!

ACUPUNCTURIST

And somebody's heart has been broken, too! Larry, you need love in your life!

LARRY

Yes! I've been trying to get back together with my ex-wife.

ACUPUNCTURIST

No... no ex-wife... Holly take care of your heart now.

LARRY

You really think so? Is it time for me to move on? Holly does seem like a great girl.

ACUPUNCTURIST

How about we let acupuncture decide?

He opens a dresser drawer and pulls out some needles. He quickly throws one of the needles into Larry's forehead.

Larry speaks dreamily.

LARRY

Ohhhhh... that feels really good... more needles please...

The acupuncturist hurls more needles into Larry's scalp, face, and neck.

LARRY
Ohhhhh... that feels incredible...

ACUPUNCTURIST
Close your eyes... put your mind in peaceful place.

Larry closes his eyes.

The acupuncturist turns on the stereo and very relaxing sounds fill the air. There is the sound of ocean waves and quiet ambient music.

The acupuncturist reaches into a jar and throws silvery dust into the air. It sprinkles down onto Larry.

LARRY
What is that? It smells like the beach!

ACUPUNCTURIST
Oh ya, I trap a little beach in a bottle!

LARRY
It smells so real! I can almost feel the ocean breeze!

The dog jumps from the dresser onto the acupuncture table. He growls and starts biting at Larry's arm. GRRRRRRRRR!

Larry is completely relaxed, and squints his eyes open.

LARRY
Ohhh, hey there little fella! Is this part of the treatment? The dog? Because I wouldn't have thought I'd like being bitten, but I reeeaallly do. This feels sooo good.

ACUPUNCTURIST

Ha! He find you delicious!

The dog starts tearing up Larry's shirt. Bits of the shirt go flying everywhere.

LARRY

Wheee! Hey little doggy! Wow, you're really tearing up my shirt! You're making beautiful confetti! I'm just gonna rest my eyes for a minute...

Larry closes his eyes and drifts off to sleep.

DISSOLVE TO:

49. Ext. Yacht - Daytime

Larry is sitting on the deck of a yacht which is sailing on the ocean. He has long flowing locks of dark Spanish hair, and he is playing a ukulele. There is a convertible parked on the deck behind him.

Holly appears next to him and runs her fingers through his beautiful head of hair.

HOLLY
I want you to be with me, Larry.

Larry smiles at her.

LARRY
I want to be with you, too.

HOLLY
Yay! Let's celebrate with sausage pizza!

A lunchroom table appears with sausage pizza on it.

Lydia appears on the other side of Larry. She strokes and caresses Larry's hair.

LYDIA
I'm sorry, Larry can't be with you. He's chained to me.

Larry looks down and his foot is chained to Lydia's foot.

LARRY
It's true. I'm chained to her.

The skeleton from Lydia's porch suddenly appears. It points at Larry and laughs.

Holly shouts at Lydia.

HOLLY
You're the one who hurt my Larry! He's mine now!

Lydia shouts back at Holly while she yanks Larry's hair.

LYDIA
Larry made a vow to me!

Holly yanks Larry's hair back towards herself.

HOLLY
Larry's my destiny!

Lydia pulls Larry's hair harder.

LYDIA
He's coming back home with me!

Holly pulls Larry's hair even harder.

HOLLY
No, he's coming home with me!

LARRY
Ladies! Please stop! There's no need to fight!

The skeleton cackles with glee.

Holly bends over and licks Larry's neck, and then she starts nibbling at his chin.

HOLLY
You're mine!

Lydia responds by licking Larry's ear, and then she begins nibbling his ear.

LYDIA
No, you're mine!

Holly grabs Larry's hair with her teeth and starts pulling.

LARRY

Ow! What's with the teeth?

Holly is growling and biting his hair, trying to pull it off his head.

HOLLY

Grrrrrrrr! Grrrrrrr!

Lydia responds by growling and biting Larry's hair as well.

LYDIA

Grrrrrrr! Grrrrr!

LARRY

Ow! What the hell?

Both women are growling and pulling at Larry's hair with their teeth. It's a tug of war.

HOLLY

Grrrrrrr!

LYDIA

Grrrrrrr!

LARRY

Ow! My hair!

CUT TO:

50. Int. Acupuncturist's Apartment - Night

Larry wakes up on the acupuncturist's table. The needles are all gone from Larry's head.

The dog is growling and has Larry's hair in his mouth. GRRRRRRRR! GRRRRRRRR! The dog is yanking Larry's hair back and forth, trying to rip the hair off of Larry's head.

The acupuncturist is desperately trying to pull the dog off of Larry.

ACUPUNCTURIST

Let go! Let go!

There is a gigantic ripping noise as the dog rips out a chunk of Larry's hair.

The acupuncturist, still holding the dog, falls backwards, knocks over a lamp, and slams against the wall.

Larry is unfazed. He speaks groggily.

LARRY

Mmmm... I've never felt so relaxed in my entire life.

Larry sits up. He is now visibly down to 75% of his hair.

The dog is playing with Larry's tuft of hair on the floor.

ACUPUNCTURIST

Awww, he so cute! Okay Larry, you all ready. Come on, get up.

Larry stands. His shirt is completely ripped up, but he looks invigorated.

LARRY

Thank you, grandmaster. I feel amazing. I feel wonderful. I feel...

Larry looks down and notices a stiff erection that is pushing up his pants like a coat hanger.

LARRY

Wow, I haven't seen that guy in a while.

ACUPUNCTURIST

Larry, you ready for love.

CUT TO:

51. Ext. Apartment Courtyard - Night

Larry looks excited. He has a big smile on his face, and he bounds up the stairs to Holly's apartment.

Larry gets to Holly's front door. He turns the doorknob, and flings open the door.

CUT TO:

52. Int. Holly's Apartment - Night

Larry springs inside Holly's apartment and shouts with enthusiasm.

LARRY
I'm ready for love!

Suddenly, Larry's face drops.

LARRY
OH. MY. GOD.

Larry is completely stunned as he sees Holly and the bouncer heavily making out with each other. Holly is topless, and the bouncer's shirt is ripped to shreds.

The bouncer tears his head away from Holly, and looks at Larry in an animalistic frenzy.

BOUNCER
OH MY GOD! This is that guy that keeps showing up! He's in your APARTMENT?! His shirt is ripped?! You LOVE ripping my shirt! This HAS to mean you're doing him!

HOLLY
How can I be doing him if I'm doing you? If anybody should be angry, it's him!

LARRY
Yeah! What's going on here?!

HOLLY

Sorry, Larry! Destiny changed! You should probably run now.

BOUNCER

You're dead meat!

The bouncer leaps for Larry.

BOUNCER

Yeeaarrgh!

LARRY

Ahhhhhhhhh!

Larry runs out the door, pulling it shut behind him. The bouncer slams face first into the door.

CUT TO:

53. Ext. Apartment Courtyard - Night

Larry carefully runs down the steps while holding onto the railing.

The bouncer runs out of Holly's apartment and jumps down the steps like an ogre.

BOUNCER

I told you tonight was the night I had to kill a guy!

He tackles Larry and they roll down to the bottom of the stairs.

The bouncer punches Larry in the face. Larry's lip splits open, and blood spurts out.

Holly is at the top of the stairs.

HOLLY

Oh, stop it, tough guy! Larry, kick his ass! Fuck him up!

The bouncer punches Larry again in the face.

LARRY

How?!

Suddenly, the acupuncturist's door opens, and the acupuncturist is holding his dog up in the air.

ACUPUNCTURIST

I can't stand a cock blocker!

The acupuncturist hurls his dog at the bouncer. The dog flies through the air and lands on the bouncer's face.

BOUNCER

AAAAAAAAHHHHHHH!

The dog is growling and tearing at the bouncer's face. The bouncer falls to the ground.

Larry gets up and runs away.

LARRY

Thank you, grandmaster!

CUT TO:

54. Int./Ext. Larry's Car - Night

Larry, in a panic, gets in his car and starts it.

The meditation flute plays, and Blue Diamond appears on the video screen.

BLUE DIAMOND
My goodness, we've never felt more powerful!

Larry drives off.

The bouncer runs out into the street after Larry, but he's too late.

He reaches down, grabs a rock, and hurls it at Larry's car. The rock shatters Larry's back windshield with a loud crash.

Larry ducks and screams.

LARRY
Ahhhh! Holy shit!

BLUE DIAMOND
So much love in the world! Can you feel it all around you?

Larry is driving frantically through the downtown streets. He looks totally beat up. He has bruises on his face, a bloody lip, ripped-up clothes, and only 75% of his hair left.

He's swerving, speeding, barely holding it together. He is hyperventilating, constantly eyeing the rearview mirror as he drives like a madman down the road.

He is barreling full speed ahead, still looking through the rearview mirror.

He then looks through the front window and sees that he is rapidly approaching the policeman, who is standing in front of some roadblocks.

The policeman is waving his arms and screaming at Larry.

POLICEMAN
STOP!! STOP!!

LARRY
Ahhhhhhhhhhhh!!

Larry slams on the brakes. The car squeals, screeches, and finally stops right at the policeman's knees.

Larry is breathing heavily, clutching the steering wheel. He rolls down his window.

LARRY
Sorry! Sorry about that!

The policeman pulls out his gun and walks over to Larry.

POLICEMAN
TURN THIS CAR OFF RIGHT NOW!

Larry turns off the car, then notices that this is the same policeman from earlier.

LARRY
Oh, hey! It's me, Larry! Remember?

POLICEMAN
Why in the hell would I know someone like you, Larry?

LARRY
Because I was with Holly?

POLICEMAN
Yeah? The only guys she hangs out with are goons and thugs. So which one are you, a goon or a thug?

LARRY
Actually, I wasn't really her type. If I could just turn around please, I'll go straight home.

The policeman shoots one of Larry's tires. The tire deflates with a hissing noise.

LARRY
That's okay, I can stay.

POLICEMAN
GET THE HELL OUTTA THE CAR!

CUT TO:

55. Ext. Downtown Street - Night

Larry gets out of the car.

The policeman points his gun at Larry. Larry puts his hands up in the air.

LARRY
I'm so sorry, officer. This was really wrong of me.

POLICEMAN
These fine people have been slaving the entire year for this one day. JUST ONE DAY that they can call their own. And you tried to plow through their dreams like a wrecking ball?

LARRY
Um... which people?

POLICEMAN
Oh yeah, why would a scumbag like you notice that there are actually other people in the world? Especially if they're a different race!

The policeman points his gun towards a Day of the Dead Festival that is right beyond the roadblocks.

In the festival, there are people of all races, but primarily Mexicans, walking around and enjoying the celebration.

A few pedestrians leaving the festival duck and scream from the policeman's gun which is pointing in their direction.

POLICEMAN

I used to be a racist just like you. But I clawed my way back to decency with a lot of personal growth in prison.

LARRY

I swear, I'm not racist. I don't even think about race.

POLICEMAN

That's the racism talking right there. So these people are just invisible to you? These fine Mexicans were once proud and dignified. But the white man has failed to appreciate their history and their culture, and the extreme sacrifices they made to build this country.

LARRY

I'm so sorry. I don't know, I just wish I could apologize to them all.

POLICEMAN

Well, you know what? That's exactly what you're going to do. You are going to GO, and you are going to apologize to EACH and EVERY person here. Apologize for almost killing them tonight. Apologize for killing their ancestors. Apologize for stealing their land and their customs.

LARRY

Won't that take a really long time?

The officer shoots another one of Larry's tires. The tire deflates with a hissing noise.

POLICEMAN
You've got nothing but time, my friend.
Come on, let me show you how it's done.

CUT TO:

56. Ext. Day Of The Dead Festival - Night

There are people everywhere, many of them dressed in a variety of skeleton costumes. Other people are wearing traditional Mexican clothing of sombreros, ponchos, and fiesta dresses.

A Mexican mariachi band is playing music. Couples are dancing. Skeleton marionettes are dancing on a table. A small parade of skeletons passes, waving the Mexican flag.

There are Mexican jumping beans and tarantulas on display. There are tarot readers with crystal balls. There are marigolds and candles surrounding photos of deceased loved ones.

Vendor booths are selling Mexican foods and drinks, Mexican crafts, ceramic skeletons, and piñatas. There are carnival rides and games.

A live chicken is walking on a piano while chicken carcasses hang from a clothesline above it.

Larry and the policeman walk up to a booth where a MEXICAN WOMAN is sitting.

The policeman points his gun at the woman as he talks. The woman looks terrified and raises her hands.

POLICEMAN

Apologize to this fine woman.

LARRY

I'm sorry.

MEXICAN WOMAN

It's okay.

POLICEMAN
What are you sorry for?

LARRY
I'm sorry for killing your ancestors?

MEXICAN WOMAN
It's okay.

POLICEMAN
And what else?

LARRY
I'm sorry for everything?

MEXICAN WOMAN
It's okay.

POLICEMAN
You don't know a thing about her. Ask her what she does.

LARRY
What do you do?

MEXICAN WOMAN
I sell dried cucarachas.

POLICEMAN
Dried cockroaches, Larry.

LARRY
Dried — cockroaches? What do you do with them?

POLICEMAN
You eat them, Larry. And you want to try them, don't you?

LARRY
Um, I wasn't really thinking about it.

POLICEMAN

But you're thinking about it now, right?
Because that's the culture!

Larry looks very frightened.

LARRY

Right, right. Maybe I'll try one?

POLICEMAN

He'll try ONE BAG.

The policeman points to a large bag of cockroaches with his gun. The woman hands the bag to Larry.

POLICEMAN

Dig in Larry, dig in. I want to see you taste the culture.

Larry slowly reaches into the bag and pulls out a large cockroach with the tips of his fingers. He just stares at it.

POLICEMAN

Put it in your mouth.

LARRY

I really don't want to do this.

The policeman pushes the gun against Larry's cheek.

POLICEMAN

Taste the culture!

Larry opens his mouth and slowly brings the cockroach closer.

He quickly throws the cockroach into his mouth and starts chewing with his mouth open.

LARRY

Aaaaaa blahh, aaaaaa blah!

We can see all the cockroach parts on his tongue. Larry is chewing and dry heaving at the same time.

LARRY

Mmmmbbbhaaa bleccccch blecccch gurkkkk!

POLICEMAN

Larry, don't you spit that out! Don't you dare!

Larry's eyes are tearing up. He is practically crying.

LARRY

Aaaaahhhhhh eewwwww blaaaaahh. Oh God!

POLICEMAN

Swallow it, Larry! Swallow it!

Larry swallows.

LARRY

GULP.

Larry's face is dripping with sweat. He is breathing heavily and clutching his chest.

LARRY

Oh God. Oh God.

The policeman starts walking away.

POLICEMAN

I'm keeping my eyes on you, Larry! I expect to see you doing this at every booth at the festival.

DISSOLVE TO:

57. Ext. Pharmacy - Night

We see the government van parked outside the pharmacy.

CUT TO:

58. Int. Government Van - Night

Inside the van, government agents are working on computers and other electronic devices.

The handcuffed pharmacist is in custody in the van, with a government agent watching over him.

The chief impatiently paces the van, and then shouts to the team.

CHIEF AGENT
Have we tracked down Larry yet? We've gotta find this guy!

The assistant comes running up.

ASSISTANT AGENT
Sorry, sir, but we're required to give our diversity hires the first crack at it.

The camera pans to reveal an old man and an old woman, slowly pecking away at their computer keyboards.

The old man suddenly stands up and begins reprimanding the wall.

OLD MAN
You rotten troublemakers! Get off my lawn before I grab the hose!

CHIEF AGENT
Jesus Christ! We don't have time for this!

ASSISTANT AGENT
Oh, also, sir, if you could please diversify the gods that you call out... it's okay to say Jesus

once or twice, but we can't be seen favoring any one deity.

CHIEF AGENT

You're gonna meet your deity right now if you don't find this guy! I already told you what to do! Triangulate his cellphone. Pull the traffic cam footage. Question everyone he might've spoken to tonight. Unleash the kraken on this guy!

The assistant scurries over to a computer and starts typing.

The chief walks up to the pharmacist while he adjusts the thinning strands of his combover.

CHIEF AGENT

You know, Kowalski, if anyone could've used priscillas for new hair, it was me! You think I didn't want to try it? Every day, I looked at that priscillas and dreamed about what I could be like with a full head of hair. Who knows how much hair potential I could've had? I could've been president by now! But no, I did the right thing. I showed incredible self-restraint because I care about the future of humanity! The fate of all mankind depends on us controlling this substance, and you're selling it like it's street drugs? Are you proud of yourself, Kowalski?

PHARMACIST

My bad! I can definitely see that now!

CHIEF AGENT

You better pray that we can clean up your mess.

The assistant comes running up.

ASSISTANT AGENT
We found him, boss! He's at the festival!

CHIEF AGENT
Let's go! Let's drive! We're closing in on you, Larry! We'll be there in 3 minutes!

ASSISTANT AGENT
Um, sir, the van's almost out of juice.

CHIEF AGENT
Jesus Christ! Why do they give us these goddamn electric vehicles?!

The assistant looks at his phone.

ASSISTANT AGENT
And there's a long line at the charging station, sir. The best I can do is 45 minutes.

CHIEF AGENT
Why aren't we charging these vans ahead of time? Do we even want to stop crime anymore? Are we even trying? Anybody?

The old man jumps up from his chair.

OLD MAN
Who moved my lawn two inches to the left?

CUT TO:

59. Ext. Day Of The Dead Festival - Night

Larry is pushing himself through the crowd, apologizing to everybody he sees at the vendor booths.

LARRY
Sorry! Hi, please forgive me. I'm very sorry.

People are looking at Larry with absolutely no idea what he is talking about.

LARRY
Sorry about the land thing! Sorry for almost killing you! Sorry about killing your families!

Larry looks back towards his vehicle, and the policeman is sternly watching him with arms crossed.

Larry approaches a fortune telling booth where there is an OLD HAG caressing a toad.

LARRY
Hello. I'm so sorry. Can you ever forgive me? Can you please give me a thumbs up so the nice policeman over there can see?

Larry does a thumbs up sign. Confused, the old hag holds out her hand with a thumbs up.

Larry looks back at the policeman. The policeman stares skeptically, shaking his head in disapproval.

The old hag speaks up.

OLD HAG

Mal cabello!

LARRY

I'm sorry, what?

OLD HAG

Mal cabello! Bad hair!

LARRY

Yes! I have very bad hair!

The old hag stands up, puts two fingers in her mouth, and whistles. She starts shouting to the vendors at the other booths.

OLD HAG

Mal cabello! Mal cabello!

Other vendors look up with excitement.

OTHER VENDORS

Mal cabello?

The vendors grab products from their booths and come running up to Larry.

OTHER VENDORS

Mal cabello?

The vendors surround Larry, encouraging him to try their products on his head.

Larry is startled at first, and then he enthusiastically responds.

LARRY

Si! Mal cabello!

BEGIN MONTAGE

Mariachi music is playing while we see Larry trying a variety of different things for his hair.

During the montage, we see:

- Different colored lotions being rubbed into Larry's head.

- Larry receiving a head massage from multiple hands.

- The old hag rubbing her toad on Larry's head. She squeezes the toad and the toad pees on his head.

- Larry eating a variety of insects, and drinking a variety of Mexican cocktails.

- Larry hanging upside down from a carnival ride that is spinning around.

- A vendor rubbing guacamole into Larry's head, and then the vendor pours sriracha on top of the guacamole and continues rubbing.

END MONTAGE

At the end of the montage, Larry is happily walking away from the festival. His hands are filled with bags of merchandise.

A crowd of people waves goodbye to Larry, and Larry waves goodbye back to them.

LARRY

Adios, mis amigos! Muchos gracias! Hasta la vista!

Suddenly, a loud, booming, deep voice is heard that thunders throughout the festival.

VOODOO PRIEST (O.S.)

WHITE MAN!

Larry shrieks and drops to the ground.

LARRY

Ahhhh! I'M SORRY!

Larry looks up, and before him stands a very tall black man, wearing an exotic collection of furs, bones, snake skins, and silks. His face has streaks of paint on it, and he has a bone through his nose. He is completely bald.

He is the VOODOO PRIEST.

Some people in the crowd fall to their knees, bowing down to the voodoo priest. Some people cross themselves. A few people clutch each other in fear.

LARRY
I'm sorry. Please don't hurt me.

VOODOO PRIEST
SILENCE!

LARRY
(whispering)
I'm sorry.

VOODOO PRIEST
No, I'M sorry.

LARRY
You are? For what?

VOODOO PRIEST
Your hair. It is falling out. I sense that you are cursed.

LARRY
Yes! All the men in my family are bald!

VOODOO PRIEST
Baldness. The worst curse of all.

LARRY
How did you know I was cursed?

VOODOO PRIEST

The spirit world tells me all. This is not natural. It is not supposed to happen to you.

LARRY

But it's already happening! I've got a whole timeline!

VOODOO PRIEST

It is because evil spirits have invaded your soul. But we can reverse this.

LARRY

Really? How?

VOODOO PRIEST

We simply need to chase the evil spirits away.

LARRY

Yes! Can you chase them away for me?

VOODOO PRIEST

Do you carry Visa or Mastercard?

LARRY

Both!

VOODOO PRIEST

Follow me.

The voodoo priest starts walking away. Larry gets up and follows him.

As they walk away, we see the policeman in the distance. Pleased with Larry's behavior, he smiles, nods his head yes, and walks away.

A few moments later, the bouncer comes running up to the same location where the policeman was just standing. His face is scratched up from the dog attack earlier.

The bouncer notices Larry's car, pounds it with his fist, and then runs into the festival.

CUT TO:

60. Int. Voodoo Temple - Night

The voodoo temple is a dark and creepy chamber with cracked stone walls that are covered with moss. Torches on the walls provide the only source of light.

The room is filled with bones, skulls, crystals, potions, and voodoo dolls with needles sticking out of them.

A group of participants is sitting on the ground in a circle with their eyes closed. They are all wearing fanciful headdresses of feathers and skulls, and have painted faces.

A few of the participants are lightly banging on bongo drums. The other participants are murmuring quietly, as if in a trance.

Larry is sitting in the middle of the circle on a wooden chair. He is wearing a large crystal necklace, and he has streaks of paint on his face.

The voodoo priest walks in carrying a cat, and places it on a stone altar. The cat meows. MEOW!

LARRY

Awww, cute kitty!

The voodoo priest holds up a large knife high above his head. The knife glistens in the glow of the torches.

LARRY

No, no, no! What are you doing?

Larry looks away, covering his eyes.

SWOOSH! The knife cuts through the air. The cat meows loudly. MEOWWWWWWWWWWWWW!

Larry is horrified.

LARRY
Oh my God, did you just kill the cat?

VOODOO PRIEST
No! I was just preparing his meal!

The camera pans to reveal a chicken breast cut in half. The cat is happily eating the chicken.

VOODOO PRIEST
What kind of person do you think I am?

LARRY
I'm sorry! I just thought —

VOODOO PRIEST
Silence! Center your soul. The ritual is about to begin.

The voodoo priest touches Larry's forehead, then closes Larry's eyes.

He picks up a stone mortar and pestle, and begins grinding dried yellow flowers into a powder.

The drums pick up in volume and intensity. The voodoo priest closes his eyes and begins to move his body to the rhythm.

The people in the circle are swaying and raising their hands upwards. They produce a low humming noise together.

CROWD
Hummmmmmmmmmmmm...

The voodoo priest speaks loudly.

VOODOO PRIEST
Makeba! Jelina! Kachango! Mubutu!

Larry opens one eye to watch the ritual.

VOODOO PRIEST
MUBUTU! MUBUTUUUUUU!

The crowd responds.

CROWD
MUBUTUUUUUU!

Larry speaks up, all on his own.

LARRY
MUBUTUUUUUU!

The drums stop. No one says anything. Everyone just looks at Larry. Larry looks around nervously.

VOODOO PRIEST
That's incredibly insulting, Larry.

LARRY
But they all...

VOODOO PRIEST
You didn't say it right.

The drums start up again and so does the humming of the participants.

CROWD
Hummmmmmmmmmmm...

VOODOO PRIEST
I call to my father! I call to his father! Open
the road that I may cross the river of death!

The voodoo priest grabs a handful of yellow powder from the mortar, and throws it at Larry's face. Larry starts coughing.

VOODOO PRIEST
Evil keeps you down! Evil lives inside of you!

The drums beat louder as the crowd chants.

CROWD
MUBUTUUUUUU!

A wind starts whipping around the room. Larry's hair stands on end. The bags of merchandise that Larry purchased get grabbed by the wind and are flying around the room like a cyclone.

The chanting gets louder.

CROWD
MUBUTUUUUUU!

VOODOO PRIEST
Evil spirits, face me if you dare!

CROWD
MUBUTUUUUUU!

The voodoo priest grabs a voodoo doll and holds it up high in one hand. In the other hand, he holds up a long needle.

VOODOO PRIEST
Speak, white man, speak! What do you want?

LARRY
I want all new hair!

The voodoo priest plunges the needle into the voodoo doll. Larry screams in pain.

LARRY
OWWWWWWWW!

Larry's body flies up off the chair as he is seized by the power of the doll.

VOODOO PRIEST
Evil spirits, reveal yourselves!

The voodoo priest twists and turns the voodoo doll.

Larry's eyes and face are unwilling, but his feet, hips, and back are whirling around the room uncontrollably.

LARRY
WHOA! WHOA!

The participants are swooning and swaying.

CROWD
MUBUTUUUUUU!

The voodoo priest bends the voodoo doll in half. Larry groans and bends over, clutching his stomach in pain.

LARRY
OHHHHHHHH!

VOODOO PRIEST
Heed my call, spirits out!

The voodoo priest twirls the voodoo doll by one of its hands. Larry's body does cartwheels and flips through the temple.

LARRY
Ahhhhhhhhh!

VOODOO PRIEST
Spirits to this room!

The voodoo priest throws the voodoo doll into the air. Larry's body goes flying up into the air and comes crashing down onto the ground.

Larry is sweating profusely and breathing heavily, as ghostly figures start emerging from Larry's body.

The ghostly figures are all the bald men from Larry's prom photo that we saw earlier in the morning.

The ghostly figures hold hands and start dancing in a circle around Larry. They speak with singsong voices.

GHOSTS
We're taking your hair! We're taking your hair!

Larry sits up on the ground.

LARRY
Oh my God! These are all my ancestors! Uncle Leroy? What are you doing here?

Uncle Leroy steps forward, while the other ghosts continue dancing around Larry.

UNCLE LEROY
I'm here to teach you a lesson, Larry! You beat the family curse, but all I ever heard from you is complaining. You had no idea how good you had it! I won the New York Marathon and people STILL spit on me because I was bald! You took it all for granted, so you SHOULD be bald! That's why we're taking your hair!

GHOSTS
We're taking your hair! We're taking your hair!

LARRY
I promise I won't take my hair for granted anymore!

UNCLE LEROY

Oh Larry, it's not just your hair. You take your WHOLE LIFE for granted. And that's why I deserve your hair! Gimme!

Uncle Leroy lunges at Larry's head and starts pulling at his hair.

LARRY

Nooooooooooo!

The other ghosts lunge at Larry as well. They're all tugging at Larry's hair.

LARRY

Stop! Stop!

The voodoo priest grabs one of the torches off the wall and starts swinging it wildly at the ghosts.

VOODOO PRIEST

Evil spirits, be gone! Be banished forever!

The ghosts begin shrieking and backing away from Larry.

The voodoo priest continues to swing the torch around Larry as the ghosts back further away.

VOODOO PRIEST

Leave this realm at once! By the shadow of the crossroads, I cast you out!

The shrieking ghosts begin dissolving, and then they all disappear with one final screech.

We hear Larry from off-screen.

LARRY (O.S.)

Oh man, it got really hot in here. I'm burning up!

The camera pans over to Larry sitting on the ground. His hair is engulfed in flames.

The voodoo priest shouts.

VOODOO PRIEST
Get the bucket of water!

Some participants grab a bucket and pour it on Larry's head. Blood pours from the bucket all over Larry.

VOODOO PRIEST
The other bucket! That's blood!

The participants grab a different bucket, and pour water onto Larry's head.

Larry's head makes a sizzling sound as a billow of smoke comes off his head.

LARRY
How does it look?! Is it bad?!

VOODOO PRIEST
It's fine, Larry. We caught it in time.

Larry's hair is completely missing from the sides and the back of his head.

Larry has less than 50% of his hair remaining. He only has one large tuft of hair left on the top of his head, and his body is drenched with water and blood.

Larry looks around the room and smiles.

LARRY
So that's it? That's what's been holding me back? That's what I needed to get out of me?!

VOODOO PRIEST

Not so fast. I sense one more spirit inside of you.

Larry's wedding ring starts shining brightly. Light emanates from the ring, filling the room. We hear a high-pitched ringing sound as the light grows brighter and brighter.

Larry holds his hand away from his body while using his other hand to shield his eyes from the blinding light.

A translucent, ghostly figure of Lydia emerges from the light. She walks gracefully towards Larry. He is tremendously excited to see her, and stands up to greet her.

LARRY

Oh my God, Lydia! I'm so happy you're here!

LYDIA

Of course, Larry! I could never leave you.

LARRY

Lydia, I've changed! I'm not boring Larry anymore! I've done all sorts of new things that I've never done before!

LYDIA

I always knew you could change! Tell me everything.

LARRY

I've had needles in my head!

LYDIA

(impressed)

No!

LARRY

I ate cockroaches!

LYDIA

How brave!

LARRY

I got my first ticket tonight! From a real policeman!

LYDIA

That is so masculine.

LARRY

I even smoked weed! Can you believe it, Lydia? Me smoking weed?! And now I'm doing voodoo! I'm a whole new man!

LYDIA

Oh, Larry! I knew you could be exciting! I never should've given up on you. Let's get back together. Let's start a family.

LARRY

Really, Lydia?! Do you mean it?!

LYDIA

Absolutely!

LARRY

And you're not just telling me what I want to hear?

LYDIA

I'm ABSOLUTELY telling you what you want to hear!

LARRY

But Lydia, look. My hair's gotten worse.

LYDIA

Oh Larry, I've never cared about your hair. I can't see past your eyes. Your beautiful blue eyes.

LARRY

This is wonderful!

Larry turns to the room.

LARRY

We're getting back together, folks! And this time it's forever!

The participants speak up in disapproval.

CROWD

- Mmm-mmm... she dead, Larry.
- Let her go.
- Time to move on.

LARRY

No no no, she's not dead. Aren't you listening? We're getting back together! I fixed it! And it doesn't matter that I'm going bald!

VOODOO PRIEST

White man, please listen...

Larry turns back to Lydia.

LARRY

Welcome back, sweetie. I've missed you so much.

Larry embraces Lydia. She leans in to kiss him. Larry puckers up and leans in for the kiss.

All of a sudden, Lydia evaporates and Larry is holding nothing.

Larry looks around the room, embarrassed. He laughs nervously.

LARRY
I'm... you know. Yay!

VOODOO PRIEST
Do you feel any better now?

LARRY
No, not really. Was that a successful voodoo session?

VOODOO PRIEST
The spirit world tells me no. You're not getting your hair back. And you're not getting your wife back, either. Oh, and all your merchandise caught on fire.

All of Larry's bags are sitting in a pile, charred to a crisp.

CUT TO:

61. Ext. Downtown Street - Night

The street is almost completely empty now. The festival is over, and people have mostly packed up and left. The atmosphere is quiet and melancholy. Somber music plays.

Larry walks slowly, without purpose. He looks sad, he is physically disheveled, and his hair is down to one big tuft of hair on the top of his head.

He stops at a dark storefront and stares at his reflection in the dark window. He appears to be thinking deep thoughts.

The focus changes and he sees a couple in the reflection: a young man and a young woman, sitting on a bus bench across the street. They kiss lovingly.

Larry turns around to look at the couple. The woman runs her hands through the man's full head of hair as they kiss.

On Larry's side of the street, a HAPPY HOMELESS GUY is sitting on the ground. He is bald, and he is sitting next to a grocery cart that is filled with bags of his belongings.

Larry glumly walks over to the homeless guy.

LARRY

Is this seat taken?

Larry sits down on the ground next to the homeless guy, and looks at the young couple again.

LARRY

That used to be me. Couple in love.

The homeless guy's words come slurring out like he's drunk.

HAPPY HOMELESS GUY

Huh? Cupful of blood?

The homeless guy starts searching through a dirty bag that sits on his lap.

LARRY

No, not cupful of blood! COUPLE IN LOVE. Whatever you're bringing out of your bag, please stop.

The homeless guy stops and shrugs his shoulders.

LARRY

I used to be like him. Young. Good looking. Lots of hair.

HAPPY HOMELESS GUY

Hair?

The homeless guy rummages through his bag and pulls out a bloody wig. He offers it to Larry.

HAPPY HOMELESS GUY

Twenty dollars.

LARRY

No, thank you. That wig has blood on it.

HAPPY HOMELESS GUY

Ten dollars.

LARRY

I'm fine, really.

HAPPY HOMELESS GUY

Makes you feel good. Look!

The homeless guy flops the bloody wig on his head and smiles.

HAPPY HOMELESS GUY

Woo hoo! See? I'm having fun!

The homeless guy pulls out a pair of Groucho Marx glasses, with the big nose and mustache, and puts them on his face.

HAPPY HOMELESS GUY

Look at me! I'm James Bond!

LARRY

I wish I could just throw on a costume and fake myself into happiness.

HAPPY HOMELESS GUY

Fake it til you make it! I'm a big star!

LARRY

Actually... would you mind if I borrowed your wig for a minute?

HAPPY HOMELESS GUY

Sure! Try before you buy.

The homeless guy flops the bloody wig on top of Larry's head.

HAPPY HOMELESS GUY

Can I have your autograph, Mr. Bond?

Larry smiles broadly. He stands and walks back over to the dark storefront window with his big grin plastered on his face.

Larry looks at his reflection. It's still not pretty. And now he's wearing a bloody wig from a homeless guy.

Larry's smile disappears, his lips start quivering, his eyes start welling up, and then he starts sobbing loudly and uncontrollably.

A HIPPIE in his 50s slinks up. The hippie is wearing a tie-dye t-shirt with a big red heart on it, some beads around his neck, colorful bell bottoms, and sandals.

He has long beautiful golden hair that literally glows. His hair is actually glowing as if it was a light source.

He talks in a very soothing, sincere voice.

HIPPIE

Hey baby, bad night? Man got you down?

Larry is still crying. He pulls the wig off his head and throws it onto the ground.

LARRY

Would anybody care if I wasn't here? Would anyone even notice if I was gone?

HIPPIE

The universe would notice. I would care. C'mere, baby. It's okay.

The hippie moves closer to Larry, and then puts his arms around Larry for a hug.

HIPPIE

Sometimes you just need a hug.

Larry hugs him back.

LARRY

I'm worn out. I can't go on another step. I've tried everything to get my life back.

HIPPIE

That's no way to live, brother. What's your name?

LARRY

Larry?

Larry looks up from the embrace and notices the hippie's glowing golden hair.

LARRY

Oh my God, your hair. It's so long. It's so beautiful. It's actually glowing!

Larry starts stroking the hippie's hair.

LARRY

So soft, too. It feels like silk.

Larry smells the hippie's hair.

LARRY

Mmmm... it smells delicious... like fresh coconut. I wish I had your hair.

HIPPIE

Naw, baby! You don't want my hair. THE MAN wants you to THINK you want my hair, so you never want what THE MAN has! Keep us fighting with each other while the man makes off with all the good stuff!

LARRY

The good stuff?

HIPPIE

Aww yeah, baby! There's GREAT stuff out there you're not even allowed to know about, cuz the man keeps it all for himself! Hair's just part of the scam, baby. That's how the man keeps you down.

LARRY

The man did this to me?

HIPPIE

Now you know! Hey, we better keep moving, he's watching us right now.

The hippie swiftly walks away, slinking from one building to another in order to hide from the man.

Larry anxiously looks around, then chases after the hippie.

The two of them quickly and covertly move down the street while they talk.

LARRY
The man is watching us right now?

HIPPIE
The man watches you like you watch TV.
You watch TV, right?

LARRY
Yeah?

HIPPIE
DON'T! That's how the man gets inside
your head, fills you with fear!

LARRY
I'm filled with fear!

HIPPIE
You toss and turn in your bed at night?

LARRY
I DO toss and turn!

HIPPIE
You get up to pee?

LARRY
I DO get up to pee!

HIPPIE
The man is scaring the piss outta you, baby.
Don't let the man grind you down.

LARRY

It's just... it's too late. I had everything. And now it's all gone. If I could just get new hair... but I don't even have a plan. I mean, I thought I had a plan, but...

The hippie stops walking and touches his fingers to Larry's lips.

HIPPIE

Shhh, shhhh. You aren't SUPPOSED to have a plan, baby. That's part of THEIR plan. Once you have the same hair as me, then we won't be fighting with each other anymore! And then we can turn our attention to fighting the man!

LARRY

I can get the same hair as you?

HIPPIE

Of course, baby! All my friends have got hair just like mine! You want to meet them?

LARRY

Yes! Can they help me?

HIPPIE

Baby, you can help yourself! To any hair that you'd like. You can even have hair that's longer than mine!

LARRY

Really?

HIPPIE

I've been looking to bring new brothers into the collective who want hair just like this. How does that sound, baby?

LARRY
It sounds like you're an angel.

HIPPIE
I'm gonna call you Brother Larry from now on.

LARRY
I've always wanted a brother! I've never had one!

HIPPIE
Brother Larry, I'm gonna take you to a place that's filled with love. A place where you can be truly free from the man. A place where nobody fights over hair, because everyone has hair just like this.

They stop walking in front of a marijuana dispensary which is closed for the night. The window says "Happy Good Times Marijuana Dispensary".

The hippie starts unlocking the door.

HIPPIE
Let's go inside, Larry. We're brothers now.

CUT TO:

62. Int. Mom's Living Room - Night

Larry's mom's living room looks like the command center for tracking down a serial killer.

The room is overflowing with people. Some people are working on laptops, many different phones are ringing, and people are analyzing maps & charts that are taped to the wall.

A teenager is recording Larry's mom with his smartphone. She holds up a photo of Larry, and fights back tears as she speaks.

LARRY'S MOM

Hello, Internet. My Larry is in trouble. He's missing and he has to come home! Please help me find him! Hashtag Save Larry!

The teenager stops recording.

TEENAGER

That's good. I'll get this all over social media.

The teenager runs off. Another person rushes into the room, holding a gigantic stack of flyers. The person holds up one of the flyers, which says "Missing Person!" at the top, with a photo of Larry underneath it.

PERSON #1

I'm gonna post all these flyers around town.

LARRY'S MOM

Thank you, dear! If Larry hasn't hurt himself by now, then somebody else has! He could be unconscious somewhere! He might not even remember his own name! He could be a John Doe, desperately needing a blood transfusion! And here I am with all of my blood, completely useless!

PERSON #1
Stay positive, Lucille. We'll find him.

The person runs away. Another person looks up from his laptop.

PERSON #2
I'm taking up a collection for Larry's search fund. It's up to $900 so far!

Neighbor Dan rushes up to one of the maps on the wall. The map has red X's drawn all over it. Neighbor Dan draws another red X across a hospital.

NEIGHBOR DAN
I just called Saint Vincent's. He's not there.

LARRY'S MOM
Oh, thank God. That place is a butcher shop. My Larry knows — it's gotta be Saint Mary's. Has anyone called Saint Mary's?

NEIGHBOR DAN
Yes, 3 times.

Neighbor Dan speaks to the room.

NEIGHBOR DAN
Everybody, let's call urgent care clinics next!

LARRY'S MOM
Oh my God. If Larry's in an urgent care, it's over! They're not even practicing medicine in those places! They're clown shows!

Another person walks into the room, holding a platter of smoked fish.

PERSON #3
When is this fish from? It smells a little off. You want I should get a new one?

LARRY'S MOM
I'm so sorry, I've been such a bad host. Let me make some more shmear.

Neighbor Dan interjects.

NEIGHBOR DAN
No, Lucille. You stay where you are. But we're running out of ideas. We've called all the hospitals. We've called all the morgues. We've called all the rooftop bars that have low ledges.

LARRY'S MOM
Call them all again!

NEIGHBOR DAN
Lucille, I don't think we have a choice anymore. We need to get the police involved.

CUT TO:

63. Int. Marijuana Dispensary - Night

The marijuana dispensary is dark. It has glass cabinets filled with a large variety of marijuana and marijuana accessories.

The hippie is leading Larry towards the far end of the room.

LARRY

Look at all this weed. If Lydia could see me now.

HIPPIE

Well, we started off as a little family-owned dispensary. But over the years, we've grown into so much more. You won't believe your eyes when you see it.

They approach a door on the far end of the room underneath an "Employees Only" sign. There is a buzzer, a speaker, and a camera on the wall.

The hippie presses the buzzer. A voice comes out of the speaker.

SECURITY GUARD (O.S.)

Passcode.

HIPPIE

Rabbit run.

SECURITY GUARD (O.S.)

Welcome back, comrade.

The door buzzes and the hippie opens the door.

LARRY
Comrade? I've never hung out with a comrade before!

HIPPIE
Oh, we're all comrades here, Larry.

LARRY
Am I a comrade too?

HIPPIE
Aww, yeah! You're everybody's comrade now. You believe in hair equity, don't you?

LARRY
Yesss! That's all I've ever asked for! Why does it have to be so hard?

They walk through the door, and it slams shut behind them.

CUT TO:

64. Int. Cement Hallway - Night

Larry and the hippie are standing in a cement hallway.

There is a heavily armed SECURITY GUARD standing next to a metal detector. The security guard has the same long golden glowing hair as the hippie.

Larry looks at him in awe.

LARRY
I love your hair.

SECURITY GUARD
Put your keys in the tray.

Larry removes his keys from his pocket and drops them into a tray.

SECURITY GUARD
I need to confiscate all cell phones.

LARRY
Oh, I don't actually have a cell phone right now. It's a long story.

SECURITY GUARD
Do you have any weapons?

LARRY
Me? Weapons? No!

The security guard starts patting down Larry.

SECURITY GUARD
Are you married?

LARRY

No.

SECURITY GUARD

What's with the ring?

LARRY

I, uh... used to be.

SECURITY GUARD

Think about letting go. Do you have any kids?

LARRY

No?

SECURITY GUARD

Do you have any friends?

LARRY

Um... a few?

SECURITY GUARD

Does anyone know you're here?

LARRY

Um... no?

SECURITY GUARD

Okay. You're done.

Larry walks through the metal detector, and the security guard hands him back his keys.

The hippie walks through the metal detector and continues walking down the cement hallway with Larry.

LARRY

Did you hear what that guy was asking me? What was that all about?

HIPPIE

We can't be too careful, Brother Larry. Even you could be the man.

LARRY

Oh no, I'm definitely not the man. I want what the man has!

HIPPIE

You've come to the right place then! When we're done tonight, the man's gonna want what YOU have!

They come to a wall with futuristic sliding doors.

The hippie places the palm of his hand on a biometric scanner on the wall. The doors slide apart.

They continue walking, and the doors slide shut behind them.

HIPPIE

Thirty years ago, our founder figured out what the problem is with humanity. Hair inequity.

LARRY

Yes! The hairs and the hair nots!

HIPPIE

That's right! Why should they get all the hair when so many people don't have any hair at all? Wouldn't it be way more fair if everyone's hair could be just like mine?

LARRY

Obviously!

They come to an open doorway that has red laser beams preventing people from passing through.

The hippie moves his face towards an eyeball scanner which scans his retinas, and the laser beams disappear.

They walk through the doorway, and the laser beams reactivate behind them.

HIPPIE

See, Larry, we're a group of people who believe that hair is a human right. If my brother doesn't have hair, why should I? That's how seriously we take it. If I see you without hair, I'll take it personally.

LARRY

I've been waiting all day for someone to say that to me.

They come to an elevator. There is a waist-high scanner on the wall.

HIPPIE

Excuse me, Brother Larry, but I need to scan my genitals. Please close your eyes.

LARRY

Oh! Of course!

Larry closes his eyes. The hippie walks towards the scanner and drops his pants. We see his naked butt from behind.

The elevator doors open, and then he pulls up his pants.

HIPPIE

Okay, let's go.

They walk into the elevator, and the doors close behind them.

CUT TO:

65. Int. Elevator - Night

HIPPIE

We're going 100 feet underground. We've been building this place in secret for 30 years behind the man's back. Nobody except for an exclusive group of people even knows it exists. You're one of those people now, Brother Larry.

LARRY

Why me?

HIPPIE

Because you've experienced how cold the world is to bald men, right?

LARRY

Yes! The world is FREEZING cold to bald men!

HIPPIE

Well, you're never going to feel that way again.

The hippie grabs the ends of his hair and alternates pulling down on each side in quick succession.

With each pull, the hair on his head rocks back-and-forth.

LARRY

Oh my God, that's a wig?! Your glowing golden hair is actually a wig?!

HIPPIE
That's right, baby.

LARRY
Where does it come from?!

The elevator stops, and the doors open.

HIPPIE
Brother Larry, welcome to... THE WIG MINE.

CUT TO:

66. Int. Wig Mine - Night

Larry and the hippie walk out of the elevator into a gigantic underground cave that extends as far as the eye can see.

The camera soars upward for a sweeping panoramic view of the cave, which reveals the staggering vastness of the wig mine.

It is a colossal underground cavern with a vast labyrinth of tunnels, towering rock formations, and subterranean lakes.

The only source of light in the entire wig mine are hundreds of torches which are hanging on the jagged dirt walls. But instead of being lit by fire, all the torches are lit by glowing golden locks of hair.

The wig mine is filled with men who are all wearing identical jumpsuits, and they are all wearing long, glowing, golden wigs on their heads.

There is a line of men walking into one of the tunnels with picks and machetes and empty wheelbarrows.

On the other side of the mine, men are coming out of a tunnel with their wheelbarrows overflowing with glowing golden locks of hair.

Larry is absolutely stunned.

LARRY

WHOA!! I can't believe what I'm seeing here!

HIPPIE

Told ya! That's what they always say!

LARRY
I've never heard of a wig mine before!

HIPPIE
That's because the man doesn't want you to know about free hair.

LARRY
Are those torches being lit by the hair?

HIPPIE
That's right!

LARRY
Incredible.

HIPPIE
This is the only known wig mine in North America. And it's populated by the indigenous troll creatures known as the wigmies. Their hair is naturally gold and glowing. We harvest their hair, and we turn it into wigs.

Suddenly, a cute little troll about 12 inches tall jumps out of a hole in the wall. His glowing golden hair flows off his head for many feet behind him.

The troll quickly scurries across the dirt path, and then jumps into another hole and disappears.

LARRY
I just saw one! Oh my god, they're adorable.

HIPPIE
Good eye! You're gonna be a good spotter. Come on, let's get you out of those tattered clothes and into a fresh, clean jumpsuit.

As they walk away on the dirt path, a few wigmies pop their heads out of holes in the cave walls and then quickly disappear again.

DISSOLVE TO:

67. Int. Wig Mine - Later

Larry is now dressed in a jumpsuit, and the hippie is taking him on a walking tour through the cave.

A group of other hippies is walking with them. They are all wearing jumpsuits and glowing golden wigs, and they are all holding machetes in their hands.

HIPPIE

Brother Larry, the man has been searching for the wigmies in jungles and forests and mountains. But they live right here in the caves! They never see sunlight, yet their hair still produces light! It's bioluminescence! It's amazing... life always finds a way of making light.

They walk through a chamber where a group of hippies in jumpsuits are hard at work on an assembly line.

HIPPIE

This is one of our many assembly lines. After fermenting the hair for 30 days, we wash it and dry it, then we comb it and weave it.

LARRY

This is quite the operation.

They walk down a corridor into another chamber, where hippies are packing wigs into boxes.

HIPPIE

This is our primary distribution center. We package and ship the wigs to every country where men are in need of hair.

LARRY

That's EVERY country, isn't it?

The hippie chuckles.

HIPPIE

Oh Larry, you're a bright one. It's gonna be good to have you around here.

They walk down another corridor, and the hippie opens a door in the cave wall. He motions for Larry to peek inside, where Larry sees a room filled with bunk beds.

HIPPIE

These are our sleeping quarters. You're guaranteed 8 good hours of sleep every night!

LARRY

Ha! I wish!

They continue walking down the corridor, and the hippie opens another door in the cave wall. Inside, there is a cafeteria where several hippies are chowing down.

HIPPIE

And all of our brothers are provided with 3 perfectly-balanced meals per day!

They continue walking.

HIPPIE

Nobody gets paid because you don't need money here. You're given everything you need, including friendships.

They turn a corner until they reach the entrance to a long, narrow tunnel.

A sign on the dirt wall reads: "Danger! No cell phones beyond this point! Highly sensitive area!"

LARRY
No cell phones beyond this point? I thought you confiscated all the cell phones back at the entrance?

HIPPIE
That's right, but after someone becomes a fully trusted brother, they're allowed to have their cell phone back again. We've got the fastest WiFi of any mine in America.

They walk into the tunnel.

HIPPIE
Brother Larry, our tradition here is that our new brothers get to choose their own hair for themselves. Go ahead, start peeking into holes until you spot a wigmy that you like.

Larry peeks into a hole and doesn't see anything. He walks down the dirt path to a different hole, but it's empty as well.

Larry sees a large hole much higher on the wall. He carefully climbs the wall by putting his feet into other holes, and he peers into the large hole.

Inside the hole, a family of wigmies is eating dinner at a small wooden table. They're smiling and laughing and eating rice with tiny chopsticks. They are drinking water from little wooden cups. Their glowing golden hair fills up the vast majority of the space.

Larry jumps down to the ground.

LARRY

There's a whole family in there!

One of the other hippies speaks up.

HIPPIE #2

A whole family? Get outta the way! It's harvest time!

The hippie pushes everybody out of the way and he starts climbing the wall, machete in hand.

He reaches into the hole and grabs one of the wigmies. The wigmy is screaming and struggling, while the rest of his family starts screaming as well.

Larry shouts.

LARRY

Wait wait wait! What's going on?

The hippie jumps to the ground and pins the struggling wigmy against the cave wall, holding him there by his hair. The wigmy flails his arms and legs, trying to escape.

The hippie raises his machete in the air.

In one fell swoop, the hippie swings the machete and shears all the golden hair off the wigmy.

The wigmy falls to the ground, and the hippie gathers all the hair in his arms.

The wigmy is now completely bald. He curls up into a ball on the ground and starts sobbing loudly.

Larry is outraged.

LARRY

You just took all his hair! That's not right! That hair belongs to him!

The original hippie speaks up.

HIPPIE

No, Larry, they love getting sheared! He wasn't using it anyway! We give them all the light they need with the torches.

LARRY

But it's their hair!

HIPPIE

Aw, baby, we're not heartless. It grows back in 5 or 6 years. We're just redistributing it from the hairs to the hair nots! It's for the greater good!

The other hippies start climbing the wall, and they each grab a wigmy out of the hole.

Larry starts shouting.

LARRY

No! Stop it! Leave them alone!

Larry tries pulling a few of the hippies down from the wall, but to no avail.

The hippies all jump to the ground, pin their wigmies against the wall, and lift their machetes in the air.

The wigmies are all crying and screaming and flailing.

Larry shouts.

LARRY

Nooooooooooo!

Larry charges towards one of the hippies and barrels into him.

The hippie loses his balance, dropping his wigmy to the ground as he falls onto the next hippie.

The next hippie loses his balance, too. He also drops his wigmy and falls onto the next hippie.

Like dominoes, each hippie falls onto the next one and they all fall to the ground, setting the wigmies free.

The wigmies cheer with joy, then scramble out of the tunnel with their long golden hair flowing behind them.

Just then, Larry turns around and sees one more hippie behind him. The hippie is down on his knees, and he is pinning one final wigmy to the ground.

The hippie raises his machete high in the air, and he grins with delight as he leers down at the wigmy.

Larry screams.

LARRY

Let him go!

Larry starts running at full speed towards the hippie, but he trips over the bald wigmy who is still crying on the ground.

Larry falls flat onto his stomach, but the momentum from his running keeps him sliding on his belly towards the wigmy that is pinned on the ground.

Larry's head crashes directly into the wigmy, which pushes the wigmy to safety. But Larry's head is now resting in the exact same spot where the wigmy's head was a moment ago.

The hippie's machete comes barreling down towards Larry's head. It strikes Larry's remaining tuft of hair, and shears it away.

Larry sits up slowly. His head is now 95% bald, except for a few scraggly patches of hair that remain on the top of his head.

All of the hippies angrily surround Larry with their machetes pointed towards him.

Larry is breathing heavily, cautiously eyeing the machetes.

LARRY
Um, I think I should probably go now.

The original hippie speaks up.

HIPPIE
Yeah Larry, here's the thing. You can't leave.

LARRY
What do you mean I can't leave?

HIPPIE
You've seen too much. Now that you know the secret of beautiful golden hair, we can't risk you telling the man about it.

LARRY
I promise I won't tell anybody. I just really need to get home.

HIPPIE
This IS your home now! You're going to sleep here. You're going to work here. And you're always going to be surrounded by the love of your brothers. Boys, bring in the chains.

LARRY
The what now?

Two muscular hippies walk in carrying heavy chains.

HIPPIE
We love you, Larry! But every once in a while, a new brother gets a little bit skittish. So you're gonna wear these chains until we burn out your thirst for freedom.

LARRY

No no no, I really need to get out of here. I've got a whole life out there. I can't miss out on my life.

HIPPIE

If you don't know what you're missing, are you really missing anything at all?

LARRY

Yes?

The two muscular hippies walk up to Larry and begin wrapping the thick chains around his chest and shoulders.

HIPPIE

You're gonna love it here! Everyone believes in the same mission as you! We're all fighting for hair equity!

LARRY

I've changed my mind. I'm on the side of inequity now.

HIPPIE

Oh, that's a good one, Larry. You'll need to bring that to our next open mic night.

The muscular hippies each grab one end of the chains and pull Larry towards the wall, where there are several metal anchors mounted to steel plates.

LARRY

Please! I really don't want to be here anymore!

HIPPIE

It's too late, Larry. But we've found that it helps if you never stop smiling.

The two hippies run the chains through the metal anchors and they are about to attach padlocks to the chains.

Suddenly, before they can attach the padlocks, the tunnel fills with incredibly loud screeching noises that seem to come from all directions and are echoing throughout the entire tunnel.

The hippie covers his ears. He starts shouting over the noise.

HIPPIE
Ahhhhh! It's an Amber Alert!

The muscular hippies drop the padlocks and the chains so they can cover their ears as well. The other hippies are also covering their ears.

The chains that are wrapped around Larry start unraveling and fall to the ground, setting Larry's body free.

The whole tunnel starts rumbling, and cracks begin forming in the walls and across the ground. Dirt starts falling from the walls and ceiling.

The hippie yells.

HIPPIE
Who brought their cell phone in here?!

Another hippie shouts back.

HIPPIE #3
We all did! We wanted to watch the
basketball highlights!

The walls start crumbling around them. Rocks are falling everywhere, just barely missing Larry and the hippies.

Wigmies frantically emerge from a bunch of holes. They climb down to the floor, and they scramble deeper into the tunnel. They disappear into other holes.

The camera follows the wigmies into the holes to reveal a huge interconnected network of small wigmy tunnels that lead them to safety.

Back in the main tunnel, the original hippie screams over the rumbling.

HIPPIE
Turn it off! Turn it off!

HIPPIE #3
We don't know how!

LARRY
You guys! I know how to turn it off! Go into your settings! Scroll down to Notifications!

The original hippie shouts over the noise.

HIPPIE
Brothers! Get out of the tunnel! It's coming down!

The hippies run out of the tunnel towards the exit as the falling rocks just barely miss them.

Larry begins to run after the hippies, but the ground splits from underneath him which propels Larry down into the ground.

Like a flume ride at an amusement park, Larry is flushed down into the ground as he rapidly descends through a network of tunnels.

LARRY
AHHHHHHHHHHHHHHHHHHHHHH!!!!

Water starts gushing in, which causes Larry to slide down even faster like a waterslide.

The tunnels twist and turn Larry in all directions through the wig mine as he slides down faster and faster.

LARRY
HELP MEEEEEEEEEE!

Wigmies scramble out of Larry's way, as they watch and point at Larry sliding by.

As Larry slides downward, the light oscillates between complete darkness and light from the wigmies' hair.

Larry keeps sliding until he goes shooting out of the tunnel into a pool of water in a small, dark cave.

CUT TO:

68. Int. Dark Cave - Night

Larry's body submerges underwater, and then he pops up, gasping for air and treading water.

Wigmies start popping their heads out of holes in the wall. They see Larry struggling below.

Larry treads to the edge of the water where he tries to grip onto the cave wall with his fingertips, but his fingers slip and he gets submerged underwater again.

His head pops up and he starts treading water again.

LARRY

Dear God, please don't let me die tonight. I'm not ready. I haven't fully lived yet! I'll be a different person, I promise! I won't ever care about hair ever again! Please, just give me another chance.

Suddenly, the entire cave begins glowing brighter and brighter.

Larry looks upwards.

Dozens of wigmies are climbing down the wall of the cave towards Larry, their glowing hair lighting the way.

The wigmy family that Larry saved earlier is leading the charge towards Larry.

As the wigmies get closer to Larry, their hair cascades downward, forming a glowing curtain of hair which drapes the wall of the cave in beautiful shimmering strands.

The father of the wigmy family beckons for Larry to grab onto the hair.

LARRY
Oh my God! Thank you!

Larry grabs onto as much hair as he can, and the wigmies start climbing back up the wall, their hair lifting Larry out of the water.

The wigmies keep climbing higher and higher with Larry hanging onto their hair, until Larry is face-to-face with a large hole in the wall.

The father wigmy motions for Larry to climb into the hole.

Larry crawls into the hole, lets go of the hair, and the wigmies start scrambling away.

Larry pokes his head out of the hole, and shouts upwards towards the wigmies.

LARRY
Thank you for saving my life!

The father wigmy looks down at Larry. He smiles, nods once, then disappears into a hole.

CUT TO:

69. Int. Sewer - Night

Larry is on his hands and knees in the sludge of a foul-smelling sewer.

The sewer is dimly lit with normal light bulbs. Pipes are running through the walls which are covered with graffiti. The sound of dripping water can be heard.

Larry stands up, pinches his nose, and starts walking briskly through the sludge. A rat scurries by his feet.

Larry comes to a ladder with a sign that reads "Emergency Exit."

Larry looks up and begins climbing the ladder.

CUT TO:

70. Ext. Downtown Street - Late Night

A manhole cover pops open in the middle of the street.

Larry sticks his head out of the hole, and we see a speeding car coming straight towards his head.

The car blares its horn, and Larry ducks back into the hole, just in the nick of time.

Moments later, Larry carefully peeks his head out of the hole and climbs out of the sewer.

DISSOLVE TO:

71. Ext. Downtown Street - Later

The government van drives slowly down the street and then stops a few blocks from Larry's car.

Several video cameras on top of the van rotate and point towards Larry's car in the distance.

CUT TO:

72. Int. Government Van - Late Night

The chief agent is looking at a bank of monitors, which are displaying live video feeds from the cameras.

CHIEF AGENT
We got him, boys. Now all we do is wait.

ASSISTANT AGENT
Um, boss, is that hair growing on the ground?

The chief grabs a joystick and zooms in on one of the video feeds.

CHIEF AGENT
Jesus Christ! Is this son of a bitch punking us?

CUT TO:

73. Ext. Downtown Street - Late Night

The trunk of Larry's car is dented and slightly ajar. It has glowing green gobs of priscillas dripping out of it, and the car's bumper is covered with hair.

The priscillas is dripping onto the asphalt, pooling into a gigantic puddle that spreads for several feet in all directions.

The puddle is glowing green and is completely covered with hair.

CUT TO:

74. Int. Government Van - Late Night

CHIEF AGENT
Jesus Christ! This is a catastrophe! We have a code 5 biohazard going down right now! We need to lock down the entire area! Boys, put on your hazmat suits, stat!

The chief runs over to a closet and opens it up. There are only empty hangers dangling inside.

CHIEF AGENT
Where the hell are the hazmat suits?!

ASSISTANT AGENT
Budget cuts, sir.

CHIEF AGENT
We don't have hazmat suits but we have a brand new gym at the office?!

ASSISTANT AGENT
Well, in all fairness, boss, our guys were getting a little pudgy around the middle.

CHIEF AGENT
I'm gonna PUNCH you in the middle right now! Boys, call for backup! We need backup!

A few of the agents start making phone calls.

ASSISTANT AGENT
Um, sir, it looks like our suspect has arrived.

The assistant points at one of the video monitors, where we see Larry walking up to his car.

CHIEF AGENT

Nobody go outside. It's too dangerous. The priscillas is awake. Just keep an eye on Larry until backup arrives!

The handcuffed pharmacist speaks up.

PHARMACIST

Make me a deal. I'll go talk to him for you guys, and you give me full immunity. How does that sound?

CHIEF AGENT

Don't make me gag you, Kowalski.

CUT TO:

75. Ext. Downtown Street - Late Night

Larry looks like a mangy mutt. His jumpsuit is soaking wet, he has cuts and bruises everywhere, and he only has a few sparse patches of hair remaining on his head.

Larry walks up to his car, relieved.

LARRY

Yes! You're still here! I don't care if you have flat tires, I'm driving you home right now!

He walks towards the driver's side door, then suddenly stops.

LARRY

What the...?

He walks around the back of his car, and looks at the hair growing on the bumper.

He touches and rubs the hair with his fingertips.

LARRY

My car is hairy?

He notices that the trunk is slightly ajar.

He slowly opens the trunk. As it opens, Larry's face glows green.

He is immediately overwhelmed by the bad smell. He waves his hand in front of his nose.

Inside the trunk, the jars of priscillas are completely shattered and broken.

There is a large pool of glowing green goop in the trunk, bubbling and smoking. Inside the goop are hairs. Thousands and thousands of hairs, growing all over the inside of the trunk.

LARRY

Oh my God, this stuff really works! I can't believe it! This stuff really works!

He tries to grab some of the hairs but they're firmly planted in the trunk.

LARRY

They're firmly rooted! They're not loose! And they're lush! Lush dark Spanish hairs!

He jumps for joy.

LARRY

Oh yes! This is a miracle! I'm gonna get my old life back!

Larry suddenly notices that the priscillas is dripping out of the trunk. He sees the growing puddle of priscillas on the ground, along with the thousands of hairs everywhere.

LARRY

Whoa whoa whoa whoa whoa! I'm losing it! Oh my god, I'm losing it! This is the very last batch! I need a bag, I need a bag!

Larry runs to the passenger side door and flings it open.

He frantically rummages through the glove compartment, but he doesn't find any bags.

He swings open the back door and rummages through a mess of papers, computer manuals, and computer cables. No bags.

He desperately looks around the street, and starts running in frenzied circles around the immediate area.

LARRY

I need a bag! Anything! A box! A cup! A beer bottle! Why is this street so freaking clean?!

CUT TO:

76. Int. Government Van - Late Night

ASSISTANT AGENT

What is he doing, boss? Is he on drugs?

CHIEF AGENT

Jesus Christ, this guy is a loose cannon! We need to take him out. Call in the snipers!

ASSISTANT AGENT

On it, boss!

The assistant hits a speed dial button on his phone, and puts it on speakerphone.

It starts ringing, and then a recorded voice comes on the line.

RECORDED VOICE (V.O.)

We are currently experiencing higher-than-normal call volumes. Please stay on the line, and a sniper will be with you shortly.

CHIEF AGENT

Jesus Christ!

CUT TO:

77. Ext. Downtown Street - Late Night

Larry runs back to the open trunk of his car. He is empty-handed.

LARRY

I'm running out of time!

He grabs the edge of the trunk, and looks inside at the pool of glowing green goop that is rapidly escaping.

His face glows green, and he is breathing heavily.

Suddenly, he dunks his entire head into the trunk.

CUT TO:

78. Int. Government Van - Late Night

All the government agents scream in horror.

CHIEF AGENT
Holy shit! This guy's a maniac!

The pharmacist looks terrified.

PHARMACIST
I didn't tell him to do that!

CUT TO:

79. Ext. Downtown Street - Late Night

Larry's head is submerged in the green goop.

He frantically swishes his head back and forth to cover as much of his head as possible.

He pulls his head out of the trunk, and the green goop is dripping all over his head, all over his jumpsuit, and all over the ground.

He closes the trunk, walks to the driver's side door, and gets into the car.

CUT TO:

80. Int. Government Van - Late Night

ASSISTANT AGENT
Boss! He's gonna drive away! We need to follow him!

CHIEF AGENT
He's not going anywhere. We're gonna ram our van into that car, and we're not gonna stop until he's flattened underneath our tires.

ASSISTANT AGENT
But sir, our insurance doesn't cover that anymore!

CHIEF AGENT
Get out of my way!

The chief pushes the assistant out of the way and jumps into the driver's seat of the van.

But then he notices someone outside.

It's the bouncer, slowly walking up towards Larry's car.

CHIEF AGENT
Who the hell is this idiot? He doesn't look like backup! Someone confirm his identity before I kill the both of them!

The pharmacist speaks up.

PHARMACIST
You want me to ask him for an ID? Just let me out of these cuffs!

CHIEF AGENT
Shut up, Kowalski!

CUT TO:

81. Int. Larry's Car - Late Night

Larry is sitting in the driver's seat of his car.

He looks at himself in the rearview mirror. His head is glowing green, and smoke is billowing off of it.

LARRY

I never respected you, hair. I took you for granted. But not anymore, I promise. If you come back, I'll take care of you. I'll do fun things with you. We're gonna have the time of our lives. Just please, grow.

Larry shuts his eyes and concentrates.

LARRY

Grow. Grow. Grow.

Suddenly, Larry's forehead bubbles. Visibly and audibly.

Larry opens his eyes, confused. He touches his head to figure out if the bubbling was just his imagination.

Just then, a person's body fills the driver's side window, and a fist knocks on the glass.

KNOCK KNOCK KNOCK!

Larry rolls down the window.

LARRY

Hello?

The person ducks down, and the bouncer's scratched-up face appears.

BOUNCER
There you are, you son of a bitch! I've been looking for you all night!

LARRY
No no no, tonight was just a big misunderstanding!

BOUNCER
You should have thought about that before you slept with my girlfriend! Now I'm finally gonna kill you!

Larry tries to roll up the window, but the bouncer's hand is holding down the window.

With his other hand, the bouncer makes a fist and pulls back his arm, ready to punch Larry.

Larry's forehead bubbles again, and this time it's painful.

LARRY
OWWWWWWWWW!!

BOUNCER
Dude! I haven't even touched you yet!

CUT TO:

82. Int. Government Van - Late Night

ASSISTANT AGENT
Sir, he's not one of ours!

CHIEF AGENT
That's it, boys! I'm taking them out! Brace yourself for impact!

The chief slams his foot on the gas pedal.

The van goes barreling down the street towards Larry and the bouncer.

CUT TO:

83. Int. Larry's Car - Late Night

Larry's head is bubbling like crazy.

LARRY

Oh, this isn't good. Feeling sick. Very sick.

BOUNCER

Shut up and let me kill you!

The bouncer cocks back his fist again.

The government van is speeding towards them at full speed.

Larry looks like he's about to faint. He grips onto the steering wheel to steady himself.

LARRY

Oh... oh no...

The bouncer notices Larry's bubbling head.

BOUNCER

What the...?

Suddenly, there is a massive explosion and a blinding flash of green light.

KABOOM!

Hair explodes out of Larry's head in all directions.

Larry's car bursts into pieces. The driver's side door flies off like a roadside bomb, taking the bouncer with it.

The bouncer screams as he flies through the air.

BOUNCER

Ahhhhhhhhhh!

Gigantic chunks of metal from the car shoot through the air and slam into the speeding government van.

The van swerves out of control and then flips over on its side, screeching to a halt.

CUT TO:

84. Int. Government Van - Late Night

The government agents are all knocked out, but the pharmacist is still conscious.

With his handcuffs still on, the pharmacist manages to pull himself out of the wreckage and goes running down the street.

CUT TO:

85. Ext. Downtown Street - Late Night

PHARMACIST

I'm free! Hahahahaaa! I'm free!

He runs off into the distance.

Larry is still sitting in the driver's seat of his car, gripping onto the steering wheel.

We zoom out to reveal that the steering wheel is no longer connected to anything, and the seat is now sitting on the ground.

But now, Larry has the largest, fullest, thickest head of hair ever seen on a human being. It looks like a gigantic afro with curly spikes of hair extending in all directions. His hair is so mammoth that it appears to weigh twice as much as his body.

Larry stumbles out of the seat, completely dizzy and unable to balance himself due to the enormous weight of his hair.

He collapses to the ground on his hands and knees.

Larry reaches up and touches his massive hair.

LARRY

I think it worked! I really think it worked! I need a mirror.

He sees the car's side view mirror lying on the ground just beyond the bouncer's unconscious body.

He crawls towards the mirror, and then crawls over the bouncer's body.

LARRY

Sorry. Sorry. Excuse me.

Larry grabs the mirror and looks into it. He sees the giant afro on his head.

LARRY

OH. MY. GOD. IT'S GORGEOUS!

Larry stands up and tries to balance himself.

LARRY

Whoa! Whoa!

At first, he sways dangerously, but then he extends both arms out to regain his balance.

He practices walking around, as if walking for the very first time.

Finally, he is able to move steadily, and he begins walking down the street.

CUT TO:

86. Ext. Downtown Street - Moments Later

Upbeat music plays as Larry walks down the street.

A nightclub is letting out for the night, and people start pouring out onto the street. They begin to notice Larry and his hair.

A man gives Larry a high-five.

STREET PERSON #1
Lookin' good, my man!

LARRY
Why, thank you!

Another guy pats Larry on the back.

STREET PERSON #2
Outta sight!

People start taking photos of Larry.

A SEXY WOMAN in nightclub attire skips up to Larry and smacks him on the butt.

SEXY WOMAN
Hey cutie pie! What's your name?

LARRY

Larry?

SEXY WOMAN
Can you dance, Larry?

LARRY
I can't lead, but I can follow!

She grabs Larry by the hands and starts dancing with him down the street. Larry matches her step-for-step.

It turns into a full-blown Charleston dance number, with both of them spinning, twirling, and kicking in unison.

People are running to keep up with them, while recording them on their phones.

STREET PERSON #3

Who is that?

STREET PERSON #4

They say his name is Larry!

When the dance ends, the crowd erupts into applause.

The woman kisses Larry on the cheek and skips away.

There is a hot dog cart behind Larry. The HOT DOG VENDOR runs up to Larry with a hot dog in his hand.

HOT DOG VENDOR

Hey buddy! Would you please eat one of my hot dogs?

LARRY

I'm sorry, but I don't have any cash on me.

HOT DOG VENDOR

What are you, crazy? Your money's no good here! Just let me get a photo with you while you're taking a bite!

LARRY

Okay, sure!

The vendor gives Larry the hot dog, then stands next to Larry for a selfie. Larry takes a bite of the hot dog, and the vendor snaps a photo.

Throngs of people start hurling themselves and their money towards the hot dog vendor.

CROWD

- I want what he was having!
- I'll pay DOUBLE for whatever that guy had!
- Please! I NEED one of those hot dogs!

One person grabs the hot dog out of Larry's hand, and holds it up like a trophy.

STREET PERSON #5

Bidding starts at $100!

Larry chuckles, and resumes walking down the street.

People are following Larry with their cell phones, live-streaming his every move.

When Larry gets to the street corner, there is a TRAFFIC COP who is directing traffic while the pedestrians wait.

As soon as he spots Larry, the traffic cop immediately blows his whistle and orders the cars to stop. The cars screech to a halt, and they all rear-end into each other.

TRAFFIC COP

Don't worry, sir. I've got a clear path for you.

Larry crosses the street.

LARRY

Thanks!

A group of people are pointing out Larry to their friends.

STREET PERSON #6

I need a photo with that guy!

People run up to Larry, and Larry poses with them for photographs.

The hairstylist is sitting at an outdoor patio, having drinks with his friends. He notices Larry and spits out his drink. He goes running up to Larry.

HAIRSTYLIST
Oh my God, Larry! Is that the surgery? I will ABSOLUTELY cut your shit hair! Please come back! It hasn't been the same without you!

LARRY
Of course I'll come back!

HAIRSTYLIST
Oh, thank God! I need your heat at the salon! Do you remember how you made me? You were there from the beginning when nobody else was sitting in my chair!

The crowd pushes the hairstylist out of the way, as they all try to get closer to Larry.

Larry continues strutting down the street, while people continue to take photos and videos. Larry smiles and waves to the crowd.

Larry passes by a movie scene being filmed. The DIRECTOR and the camera operator are very tight on a beautiful young ACTRESS kissing a young heartthrob ACTOR.

As Larry passes, the director taps the camera operator on the shoulder.

DIRECTOR
Follow him now! Trust me! I haven't seen charisma like that since Marlon Brando 1951!

The director and the camera operator chase after Larry while filming him, leaving behind the two confused actors.

ACTRESS
No offense, but I want to kiss HIM.

ACTOR
Me too!

The actors go running off after Larry.

Larry is grinning from ear-to-ear as he continues to stride down the street.

The voodoo priest is trying to push his way through the crowd towards Larry, but he just can't make it all the way to Larry.

VOODOO PRIEST
Please, white man, come back! I wish to make a perfume from your soul!

The voodoo priest gets lost in the crowd, as the crowd continues to surround and follow Larry.

The policeman is standing on a street corner, beaming with pride as he watches Larry walk down the street. He crosses his arms and nods his head yes.

POLICEMAN
See, Larry? This is what happens when you let people in!

A CHAUFFEUR is standing on the curb next to a limousine, holding the door open for Larry.

CHAUFFEUR
Your car, sir.

LARRY
For me?

CHAUFFEUR

Of course! Call me anytime you need a complimentary ride.

The chauffeur hands Larry his business card.

Larry gets into the limousine, pushing down on his head of hair so he can squeeze inside.

The chauffeur closes the door behind Larry and then gets into the driver's seat. The limo pulls away.

CUT TO:

87. Int./Ext. Limousine - Late Night

Larry looks outside the window of the limo. People are running after the limo, banging on the window and shouting.

CROWD
- We love you, Larry!
- Take me with you!
- Thank you for everything!

LARRY
Amazing. And all it took was some hair.

CHAUFFEUR
Shall I drive you to dinner, sir?

LARRY
Sure!

CHAUFFEUR
Right away, sir.

Suddenly, the back door opens and the handcuffed pharmacist jumps into the limo. Larry is startled.

LARRY
Ahhhhh! What are you doing here?

PHARMACIST
Hey listen, don't freak out guy, but I severely undercharged you for that stuff. I'm gonna need a couple hundred more bucks.

The chauffeur turns around.

CHAUFFEUR

Hey! No bald guys in here!

PHARMACIST

Gotta run! Catch you later!

The pharmacist jumps out of the limo and slams the door shut behind him.

The limo pulls up to a fancy restaurant.

CHAUFFEUR

Your destination, sir.

LARRY

Thank you!

Larry holds down his hair so he can get out of the limousine.

CUT TO:

88. Ext. Fancy Restaurant - Late Night

As Larry steps onto the curb, there are blinding flashes of light from the paparazzi who are taking rapid-fire photos of Larry.

Larry walks up a red carpet leading to the restaurant, and the paparazzi are shouting at him.

PAPARAZZI
- Larry! Look this way!
- Who are you dating?
- What's your next project?

Larry approaches the front door of the restaurant, where the RESTAURANT OWNER greets him.

RESTAURANT OWNER
Good evening, Larry. Your table is ready. And remember, your meals are always on the house.

LARRY
That's very kind of you!

CUT TO:

89. Int. Fancy Restaurant - Late Night

The owner leads Larry into the upscale restaurant, where all the guests are extremely dressed up.

The guests rise to their feet at their tables, and give Larry a warm, enthusiastic round of applause.

Larry waves at the crowd and then whispers to the owner.

LARRY

Um, I'm feeling a little underdressed.

RESTAURANT OWNER

Not a problem, sir.

He snaps his fingers, and two tailors come running up to Larry and start measuring him.

SPIN TRANSITION TO:

90. Int. Fancy Restaurant - Later

Larry is now standing in a full tuxedo.

RESTAURANT OWNER

My gift to you.

LARRY

It's perfect! Thank you!

RESTAURANT OWNER

Please. Follow me.

The owner leads Larry to a corner table near the window, and Larry sits down in a plush velvet chair.

A waiter brings over a silver tray with a domed cover, and places it on Larry's table. The waiter lifts up the cover to reveal a fully baked chicken.

WAITER

A fully baked chicken, sir.

LARRY

Wow. I have finally arrived.

Outside the window, crowds of people are watching and recording Larry.

The waiter pulls a red velvet curtain around Larry's table to give him privacy.

SPIN TRANSITION TO:

91. Ext. Fancy Restaurant - Later

Larry walks out of the restaurant in his tuxedo, patting his belly.

LARRY
That was delicious.

RESTAURANT OWNER
Larry, in your honor, I am changing the name of my restaurant.

The owner pulls down on a string and a banner falls over the previous name of the restaurant, which was "Chauncey's Kitchen". Now the restaurant's name is "Larry's Kitchen".

LARRY
You're too kind!

The crowd erupts in cheers. People in the crowd are wearing Larry t-shirts, Larry hats, and are waving Larry headshots.

CUT TO:

92. Ext. Downtown Street - Late Night

Larry continues walking down the street as people follow him with their phones.

Superimposed over Larry are a stream of loving social media posts about him: photos, videos, hearts, fire emojis, trending hashtags, and positive comments.

CUT TO:

93. Ext. Downtown Central Square - Late Night

Larry turns a corner and enters the downtown central square which is overflowing with people.

There is a gigantic digital billboard live-streaming Larry's every move. It says "LarryStream", and an online influencer is speaking onscreen.

ONLINE INFLUENCER
And remember, you can support LarryStream by ordering our exclusive merch! We've got a new Larry jersey, and yes, a brand new Larry doll! That's right, folks, you heard it here first — a Larry doll!

The influencer holds up a Larry doll onscreen.

In the downtown square, Larry waves and the crowd cheers. He signs autographs and takes more photos with his fans.

We see Larry's boss pushing through the crowd towards Larry. He is carrying the HR Guy on his back.

BOSS
Oh my God, Larry! Look at those beautiful locks! I knew you were holding the line, but you're more than holding the line! You've transcended the line!

The boss puts the HR guy onto the ground.

BOSS
I want his salary doubled!

The HR guy shakes his head no, and holds up 4 fingers.

HR GUY
Nuh-uh! Nuh-uh!

BOSS
You're right! We need to quadruple his salary!

The HR Guy makes a big circular gesture with his hands, like he's outlining the whole world.

HR GUY
Eh eh eh! Eh eh eh!

BOSS
Oh my God, you're right! Larry, take my keys. The business is all yours.

The boss hands Larry his keychain.

LARRY
Aren't the keys to your house on here?

BOSS
It's a beach house. You'll love it.

LARRY
No, I couldn't possibly...

BOSS
Take it! I've been looking for a superstar like you to become my successor! You are my legacy!

The HR Guy gives a big thumbs up and hops onto the boss' back. The boss starts walking away.

BOSS
I'll see you first thing Monday morning for the official transition meeting!

Larry is speechless, when suddenly a loud noise erupts from overhead. People start running out of the way as a helicopter lands in the square.

The yacht guy opens the helicopter door and shouts through a megaphone.

YACHT GUY

Welcome to the good life, my fellow hair!
Hop aboard!

SPIN TRANSITION TO:

94. Int. Helicopter - Late Night

Larry is sitting next to the yacht guy on the helicopter, which is flying over the city.

YACHT GUY

My god, man! You look fantastic! But which one of us is more fantastic? I challenge you to a yacht race!

LARRY

I don't have a yacht!

YACHT GUY

I'll lend you one of mine! Come on!

SPIN TRANSITION TO:

95. Ext. Lake - Late Night

Larry and the yacht guy are racing 2 yachts side-by-side down the lake. Larry is ecstatic.

LARRY

Wooo hooo!

The yacht guy shouts over to Larry's yacht with his megaphone.

YACHT GUY

Come on, Larry! Faster, you pussy, faster!
Hahahahaha!

CUT TO:

96. Ext. Downtown Central Square - Late Night

The yacht race is being live-streamed onto the LarryStream billboard.

People are waving Larry flags and cheering.

CROWD

- Go Larry!
- Lar-ry! Lar-ry! Lar-ry!

CUT TO:

97. Int. Mom's Living Room - Late Night

A police detective is talking to Larry's mom in her crowded living room. She looks very distressed.

POLICE DETECTIVE
We'll put out an Amber Alert right away, ma'am.

Suddenly, Neighbor Dan comes running up to Larry's mom and points at the television.

NEIGHBOR DAN
Lucille! You've gotta see this!

She turns around to look at the TV and sees Larry racing the yacht.

At first she is shocked, and then she bursts into tears of joy.

LARRY'S MOM
My boy! He's alive! My precious boy is alive! And — oh my God — he really beat the curse!

On the television, Larry's yacht speeds towards a giant banner that reads "Finish Line" and he crosses the finish line first.

Everyone in the living room starts celebrating. People are cheering and applauding and high-fiving each other.

Everybody surrounds Larry's mom for a gigantic group hug.

The detective interrupts.

POLICE DETECTIVE

Ma'am, do you mind if I grab some more shmear on my way out?

CUT TO:

98. Ext. Yacht - Late Night

On Larry's yacht, people are popping champagne bottles and throwing confetti in the air.

The yacht guy jumps onto Larry's yacht, and he hands Larry a trophy.

YACHT GUY

Oh well, Larry, you won my trophy. "Most fantastic man on the planet." I'm sorry to see it go, but you're the rightful owner.

LARRY

Aww, thank you!

YACHT GUY

And Larry, there is one more thing... this yacht is now yours!

LARRY

No way! Where am I gonna store a yacht?

YACHT GUY

Don't worry about it. I'll tell you everything next week at the country club!

SPIN TRANSITION TO:

99. Ext. Downtown Central Square - Late Night

The helicopter drops off Larry back in the central square. He holds up his trophy, and the crowd roars.

Several women push their way through the crowd and surround Larry.

They are grabbing at Larry's hair, and each one is trying to get his attention.

WOMEN
- Call me, Larry!
- I want your babies!
- You're my soulmate!

The women start pushing and fighting each other.

STREET WOMAN #1
Get in line!

STREET WOMAN #2
I was here first!

STREET WOMAN #3
He would never be with you sluts!

LARRY
Whoa whoa whoa! Ladies, calm down!

CUT TO:

100. Ext. Downtown Street - Late Night

On the street, cars and tour busses are backed up in heavy traffic to catch a glimpse of Larry.

Lydia is sitting on the back of Alejandro's motorcycle in the traffic jam.

Alejandro is trying to get around the traffic, but they are stuck.

Lydia is getting impatient.

LYDIA

What is with all this traffic?

She suddenly notices Larry in the distance.

LYDIA

Larry?

She jumps off the motorcycle.

ALEJANDRO

Lydia! Where are you going?

LYDIA

I'll meet you back home!

Lydia goes running into the downtown square.

ALEJANDRO

Lydia?

CUT TO:

101. Ext. Downtown Central Square - Late Night

More women have surrounded Larry and are fighting over him.

A beautiful woman grabs both of Larry's arms to get his attention. She is SUSIE JORGENSEN.

SUSIE JORGENSEN
Larry, it's me! It's Susie Jorgensen! Your high school sweetheart!

LARRY
Susie? Oh my God! How are you? It's been so long!

SUSIE JORGENSEN
I'm sorry I stood you up on prom night. I feel so stupid.

LARRY
You didn't stand me up! You got food poisoning! It wasn't your fault!

SUSIE JORGENSEN
No, Larry. I have to tell you the truth. I drove up to your house that night and I saw you standing out front with all of your bald relatives. I freaked out. I was terrified that our future children would all be bald! So I drove off — and then I broke up with you.

LARRY

What?! You broke up with me because of baldness? Susie, we were in love with each other! We were gonna get married!

SUSIE JORGENSEN

I know! I was wrong! Will you please forgive me? And will you marry me now?

She grabs Larry's face and starts kissing him passionately.

Suddenly, Lydia appears. She grabs Susie by the hair, and pulls her face away from Larry.

LYDIA

Get your mouth off my husband, you whore!

SUSIE JORGENSEN

Ow! What the hell?

Larry's eyes light up.

LARRY

Lydia?! What are you doing here?

Lydia shouts to the crowd.

LYDIA

He's married to me! Look at this!

Lydia grabs Larry's hand and holds it up to show all the women his wedding ring.

Susie Jorgensen shouts at Lydia.

SUSIE JORGENSEN

You're not his wife! You're not wearing a ring!

LYDIA

It's getting cleaned, bitch!

Lydia pushes Susie, and Susie pushes her back.

All the women, including Lydia, start fighting with each other. They are pushing each other and grabbing each other's hair. It's a full-blown catfight.

All of a sudden, Lydia whips out a gun from her purse and fires it into the air.

LYDIA
Back off, bitches! He's mine!

The women scream. Some of them dive to the ground. Other women run away.

LARRY
Lydia! When did you get a gun?

LYDIA
I've changed, Larry.

LARRY
I've changed, too!

LYDIA
Come on, follow me!

Lydia grabs Larry by the hand, and they start running through the downtown square.

As they run, Lydia shoots a few more times into the air.

CUT TO:

102. Ext. Downtown Alley - Late Night

Lydia leads Larry into a quiet, deserted alley.

Lydia throws her purse to the ground, pushes Larry up against a brick wall, and starts kissing him intensely.

Larry throws his trophy to the ground, wraps his arms around Lydia, and passionately kisses her back.

Lydia runs her fingers through Larry's hair while she makes out with him. She purrs with delight.

In between kisses, she speaks breathlessly.

LYDIA
Oh, Larry! I want you back! I want you to move back in!

LARRY
Yes! Of course I'll move back in!

LYDIA
I'm sorry I've been such a selfish bitch.

LARRY
No, you're not a bitch! You're a really good person!

LYDIA
I want you so badly. Let's make a baby right now!

While kissing Larry, Lydia pulls off her shirt and throws it to the ground. She reaches behind her back, unhooks her bra, and tosses it aside, leaving her topless.

LARRY

Whoa! Lydia, we're in public!

LYDIA

I don't care! I need you right now! You are so hot. And your hair is to die for.

She kisses his neck while unbuttoning Larry's tuxedo pants and pulling down his pants.

LARRY

I did it just for you! I knew you would fall back in love with me if I got all new hair!

LYDIA

No, Larry, I would feel this way about you even if you had absolutely no hair at all! You're a completely different person now! You've changed on the inside!

LARRY

I really have changed! You're gonna love the new Larry!

LYDIA

I already do. I love you, Larry! I love you, I love you, I love you!

LARRY

I love you too, Lydia! I love you too! This is the best day of my entire life!

Suddenly, all of Larry's hair falls out at once. There is a gigantic FWOP noise as all the hair hits the ground. The entire alleyway is covered with hair.

Larry's head is completely and totally bald. It's all gone. Not even the faintest sign of even a single strand of hair. There is absolutely nothing left. His head is as smooth and shiny as a bowling ball.

Larry's eyes go wide in shock. He puts his hands on his head for confirmation that he is, indeed, completely bald.

LARRY
(stunned)
All go bye-bye?

Lydia gasps in horror and covers her boobs.

LYDIA
What the hell is this? Is this some sort of a joke?

LARRY
No no no, I didn't know this would happen...

LYDIA
(disgusted)
Oh God, Larry. I knew you could never change.

LARRY
But you just said —

LYDIA
Same old Larry.

She grabs all of her belongings off the ground, and storms out of the alley in disgust.

As she leaves, we see her making a phone call.

LYDIA
Alejandro! Come pick me up immediately!

Larry yanks up his pants and yells after Lydia.

LARRY
You know what, Lydia?! Everyone was right! And now I finally see it! You really are a

bitch! I'm done with you, Lydia! I don't need you anymore! I'm gonna live my best life without you! I'm going to be happy without you! And one thing I know for sure! I never want to see this ring again!

Larry rips the wedding ring off his finger and throws it down the street.

Everything is completely silent except for the sound of the wedding ring clinking on the cement as it bounces down the street.

The wedding ring rolls into a sewer grate and disappears.

Larry is breathing heavily, and it looks like he is about to cry.

Suddenly, Larry's head bubbles a little bit. He grabs his head in pain.

LARRY

Owwwww!

From Larry's point of view, we can see that he is seeing double of everything, along with streaks of green.

LARRY

Whoa, I gotta take it easy.

Larry's head bubbles again. He starts getting dizzy, and he grabs onto the brick wall to hold himself up.

LARRY

Oh God, I don't feel so good...

Larry's head bubbles some more. He groans in pain again.

LARRY

Ohhhhh...

Larry's head is bubbling like crazy.

LARRY

I need help.

He tries to take a few steps to find help, but his eyes roll back in his head and he collapses to the ground.

His head hits the ground, and he is knocked unconscious.

DISSOLVE TO:

103. Ext. Clouds In The Sky - Daytime

Larry's eyes are closed.

He opens his eyes, and he is standing on a patch of clouds in the sky. He is still completely bald.

Ahead of him in the distance, a man sits on the clouds, facing Larry.

Larry starts walking towards the man.

CUT TO:

104. Ext. Downtown Alley - Late Night

The angry homeless guy from earlier in the morning is standing over Larry's unconscious body.

He grabs a stick out of his grocery cart and pokes Larry. The body doesn't move.

CUT TO:

105. Ext. Clouds In The Sky - Daytime

Larry walks towards the man who is peacefully sitting on the clouds.

It is Blue Diamond.

Blue Diamond is wearing his elegant blue robe covered with sparkling blue diamonds. Blue light is glowing from his body. His long, flowing white hair spills onto the clouds around him.

Larry walks incredulously towards Blue Diamond, who speaks in a calm, soothing voice.

BLUE DIAMOND
Hello, Larry.

LARRY
Blue Diamond! What are you doing here?
Are you God? Wait, am I dead?

Blue Diamond chuckles.

BLUE DIAMOND
Please, Larry. Have a seat.

Larry sits down on a cloud.

BLUE DIAMOND
Have you been running around all night, trying to get new hair? You don't need it. Let it go.

LARRY
That's easy for you to say. Look at all your hair.

BLUE DIAMOND

I'm not going to lie. Having hair like mine is freaking awesome. But you can't control your hair. You can only control your attitude. Choose happiness.

LARRY

How can I be happy when I've lost everything good in my life?

BLUE DIAMOND

The secret to happiness is gratitude! You already have what you need to be happy. You just need to stop taking everything for granted.

LARRY

No, that's not true! I had it all tonight and I didn't take it for granted! I was so grateful for all of it!

BLUE DIAMOND

Oh Larry, it's easy to be grateful when you have everything. It's much harder to be grateful when you have nothing.

CUT TO:

106. Ext. Downtown Street - Late Night

The angry homeless guy is pushing his grocery cart down the street.

Inside the grocery cart is Larry's unconscious body.

CUT TO:

107. Ext. Clouds In The Sky - Daytime

LARRY

What can I possibly be grateful for? I've never been more miserable in my entire life.

BLUE DIAMOND

You'll stop being miserable as soon as you stop complaining about your life, and start noticing the little things to be grateful for instead. Be grateful that you're alive. Be grateful that you have a roof over your head. Be grateful that you have friends who care about you. And be grateful that you still have time to find the next love of your life.

LARRY

Oh my god, you're right. I was the bitch all along!

BLUE DIAMOND

That's right, Larry. You've been the bitch this whole time.

LARRY

I didn't know that gurus were allowed to say bitch.

BLUE DIAMOND

Oh, behind the scenes, we all talk like this. You should have heard Gandhi.

CUT TO:

108. Ext. Downtown Street - Late Night

The angry homeless guy pushes the grocery cart containing Larry's body into a doorway.

A hand comes out of the doorway and gives the homeless guy a hundred-dollar bill.

CUT TO:

109. Ext. Clouds In The Sky - Daytime

BLUE DIAMOND

So remember, Larry, your life doesn't need to be perfect for you to be grateful. But once you are grateful, your life will feel like it's perfect.

LARRY

I understand, Blue Diamond. I'll get started right away.

BLUE DIAMOND

Good. Go live what you've learned. Namaste.

LARRY

Namaste, Blue Diamond.

We hear the sound of the meditation flute.

BLUE DIAMOND

Now close your eyes and breathe.

Larry closes his eyes and takes a deep breath.

BLUE DIAMOND

On the count of 3, you'll wake up feeling peaceful and refreshed. One, two, three.

We dissolve to a closeup of Larry's smiling face.

Larry calmly opens his eyes, and then his face turns to horror.

LARRY
Oh my God! What the hell is going on?!

CUT TO:

110. Int. Creepy Surgery Room - Unknown Time

Larry is completely naked. His body is lying stiffly on a grimy surgical table like a corpse.

The room is illuminated by fluorescent lights that are flickering and buzzing. There are blood stains splattered on the walls.

A wooden workbench is covered with rusty knives and other sharp tools.

Above the workbench, a shelf displays glass jars filled with human organs floating in formaldehyde. We see a brain, heart, liver, kidney, and eyeballs.

A tall woman wearing a white lab coat is hunched over the workbench. She is the SKETCHY DOCTOR.

She turns around to face Larry, and speaks in a perky voice.

SKETCHY DOCTOR
Oh, Larry! You're awake! I must not have used enough sedative.

Larry notices that her white lab coat says "Harvard Department of Surgery".

LARRY
Where am I? Is this Harvard?

SKETCHY DOCTOR
No, silly! You're not at Harvard. *I* was at Harvard, many years ago. YOU are in my basement.

LARRY
Why can't I move my body?!

SKETCHY DOCTOR
Oh, it's just a little splash of horse tranquilizer to keep you relaxed. I can't have my patients squirming around while I'm harvesting their kidney.

LARRY
What are you talking about?! You can't take my kidneys!

SKETCHY DOCTOR
Not KIDNEYS, Larry. KIDNEY. Singular. I always leave my patients with a spare.

LARRY
Help! Somebody! Get me out of here!

Larry's paralyzed arms begin to tremble, and then they go rigid again.

SKETCHY DOCTOR
Oh, Larry, calm down. There's no need to worry about your kidney, because I've changed my mind. I'm cutting off your balls instead!

LARRY
What? You can't cut off my balls!

Larry's hands briefly clench into fists and then open up stiffly again.

The sketchy doctor grabs a bloody hatchet from her workbench and starts sharpening it on a slab of granite.

SKETCHY DOCTOR

Larry, this is your lucky day! We're going to cure you of your baldness! While you were sleeping, I heard you mumbling about wanting new hair, and that reminded me of why I got into medicine in the first place! I got into medicine because of Papa! My papa used to mumble like that in his sleep after he went bald. Can you imagine how sad his little girl was who had to listen to that every night? That little girl was me, Larry. This is about that little girl's sadness. I promised Papa that I would find the cure for baldness, but somewhere along the way, I forgot my mission.

LARRY

What the hell does that have to do with my balls?!

Larry's fingers start to wiggle, and then they freeze up again.

SKETCHY DOCTOR

Don't interrupt me, Larry. Things get very messy when I'm angry. Anyway, while I was at Harvard, I figured out why men go bald and most women don't. Testosterone. Too much testosterone leads to baldness! If you wanna fix the problem, you've gotta go straight to the source. The testicles! It's so simple! You just cut off the balls and the hair sprouts right back! I wrote my entire thesis on it, but as soon as those ingrates at Harvard read my paper, they locked me out of the entire medical system! Globally! They called me crazy. Can you believe it?

LARRY

Yes! Somebody, help me! Please!

Larry's legs begin twitching, and then they abruptly stop moving.

SKETCHY DOCTOR

Oh Larry, they always call geniuses crazy at first. But you, Larry — you are my shot at redemption! I'm gonna prove those bastards at Harvard wrong! After your testicles are gone and you grow a beautiful new head of hair, they'll have no choice but to take me back. I'm gonna get my old life back! I'm gonna be happy again! You do want me to be happy, don't you, Larry?

LARRY

Listen, listen, listen! I learned something very important today. True happiness doesn't come from wishing that your life had turned out differently. True happiness comes from being grateful for the life you currently have!

SKETCHY DOCTOR

Oh, Larry, that's just the testosterone talking. You're a testosterone addict! It's time to end your addiction.

The sketchy doctor leans over Larry's crotch and raises the hatchet high in the air.

Larry shouts.

LARRY

Nooooooo!

Larry's leg suddenly springs to life, and it kicks the sketchy doctor directly in her face.

SKETCHY DOCTOR

Ahhhhhhhhh!

Blood spurts from her nose, as she drops the hatchet and goes stumbling backwards.

She crashes into the workbench, which tips over and sends the tools clattering to the ground.

The workbench smashes into the shelf holding the jars of human organs, causing it to collapse.

The jars shatter on the ground, spilling organs and formaldehyde across the floor.

Larry's arm jolts awake and he pushes himself off the surgical table. He falls to the ground with a thud.

Larry starts crawling towards the door.

The sketchy doctor grabs a chainsaw from the pile of tools on the ground.

SKETCHY DOCTOR

Oh, you ungrateful little baldie!

She revs up the chainsaw.

SKETCHY DOCTOR

That bald head is staying with me!

She runs towards Larry with the chainsaw, right as Larry manages to stand up and grab onto the door handle.

Suddenly, the sketchy doctor slips on a kidney. She falls to the ground and the chainsaw goes sliding across the floor towards Larry.

Larry picks up the chainsaw, turns it off, and stands up tall and proud.

LARRY

This bald head is mine — and I love it!

Larry opens the door. Sunlight floods the room as he steps outside.

CUT TO:

111. Ext. Downtown Street - Sunrise

Bald and naked, Larry emerges onto the downtown street, carrying the chainsaw in front of him.

The sun is beginning to rise. Larry smiles and takes a deep breath.

Just then, a FEMALE PEDESTRIAN walks around the corner and bumps into Larry.

She looks down at the chainsaw and starts screaming.

FEMALE PEDESTRIAN
Ahhhhhhhhhh!

LARRY
Oh no no no! This isn't mine!

Larry throws the chainsaw onto the ground, which exposes his genitals to the woman.

LARRY
Uh-oh.

FEMALE PEDESTRIAN
You bald naked pervert!

She starts whacking Larry with her purse.

FEMALE PEDESTRIAN
You sick, bald freak!

LARRY
No, you don't understand!

FEMALE PEDESTRIAN

Somebody, call the police!

Above them, an apartment window opens up. A man sticks his head out the window.

APARTMENT MAN

What the hell is going on down there?

FEMALE PEDESTRIAN

This bald lunatic just attacked me!

APARTMENT MAN

Is that Larry?

LARRY

No! It's not me!

Larry starts running down the street. The apartment man yells.

APARTMENT MAN

Don't let him outta your sight!

The woman starts running after Larry, yelling to other pedestrians.

FEMALE PEDESTRIAN

Stop that bald monster!

A few people shriek and cover their eyes when they see Larry's naked body running past them.

Other people begin chasing Larry.

CROWD

- Get back here, you creep!
- Larry, you're a sicko!
- Somebody tackle him!

Larry runs by a park, where a group of hippies from the wig mine are smoking weed.

HIPPIE #2

Hey, that's Brother Larry!

HIPPIE

No, that's TRAITOR Larry! Get him!

The hippies pull out some knives and start running after Larry, joining the group of people who are already chasing him.

Larry runs by a hospital, where Holly is pushing the bouncer in a wheelchair. He is in a full body cast.

Holly notices Larry running by.

HOLLY

How dare you, Larry! You did this to my boyfriend!

Holly runs after Larry, leaving the bouncer behind.

BOUNCER

No, don't leave me again! You promised!

The bouncer's wheelchair goes rolling backwards down a hill.

BOUNCER

Ahhhhhhhhhh!

The growing crowd continues to chase Larry.

While running, Larry sees the hairstylist sitting at an outside cafe, drinking and laughing with a group of stylish friends.

Larry shouts out to the hairstylist.

LARRY

Please help me! Tell them I'm a good person!

One of the stylish friends is shocked.

STYLISH FRIEND
Do you know that bald freak?

HAIRSTYLIST
Absolutely not!

The hairstylist shields his face with a menu as Larry runs past.

Dozens of people are now chasing Larry.

CROWD
- You tricked us, Larry!
- You're disgusting!
- You bald scumbag!

Lots of people in the crowd are recording Larry with their cell phones as they run after him.

Larry runs by the hot dog vendor, where an angry crowd of people are toppling over his cart.

The vendor shouts.

HOT DOG VENDOR
I swear, I just met the guy tonight!

Larry runs by a cemetery, where the voodoo priest is digging up a grave. He begins sniffing the air, then notices the mob chasing Larry.

VOODOO PRIEST
White man! I smell evil spirits chasing you!
You must make an offering to the Gods!

LARRY
I don't have anything to offer!

VOODOO PRIEST
Then keep running!

Larry runs by the fancy restaurant, where a crowd of people are throwing rocks through the window.

The employees are pulling down the banner that says "Larry's Kitchen". The restaurant owner yells at them.

RESTAURANT OWNER
Get rid of it! Faster! Before they kill all of us!

Larry looks over his shoulder in fear and runs even faster.

The acupuncturist is doing tai chi on the grass with his dog, when he notices the uproar.

ACUPUNCTURIST
Larry! Where your hair go? That not acupuncture fault!

LARRY
No, it's my fault!

Superimposed over Larry are a stream of negative social media posts about him: comments calling for Larry to be canceled, memes showing Larry behind bars, vomit emojis, thumbs-down emojis, and lots of angry-face emojis.

CUT TO:

112. Ext. Downtown Central Square - Sunrise

Larry turns a corner and runs into the downtown central square.

People are ripping up their Larry headshots and throwing their Larry merchandise into the trash.

The gigantic digital billboard is live-streaming Larry running naked through the streets.

The screen reads "Warning: Larry on the Loose!", and the online influencer appears onscreen.

ONLINE INFLUENCER
Just to be clear, folks, we do NOT support Larry! We have NEVER supported perverts or con-artists! We fully denounce Larry!

He holds up a Larry doll, and sets it on fire.

Larry's boss and the HR guy are playing hopscotch. The HR guy notices Larry running by, and starts pointing frantically at Larry.

HR GUY
Nuh-uh! Nuh-uh!

The boss sees Larry and starts yelling at him.

BOSS
You're fired! You're a bald loser! Holding the line, my ass! I want my keys back!

The boss and the HR guy join the gigantic crowd to run after Larry.

The helicopter appears overhead and the yacht guy shouts through his megaphone.

YACHT GUY

You're not fantastic, Larry! You're a jerk! If you think you're getting that yacht, you've got another thing coming!

He holds up a remote control and presses a big red button on it. In the distance, a yacht explodes.

CUT TO:

113. Int. Mom's Living Room - Sunrise

Larry's mom is smiling and laughing with everyone in her living room. People are eating food, and drinks are flowing.

Suddenly, Neighbor Dan shouts to Larry's mom.

NEIGHBOR DAN
Lucille! You need to see this!

Larry's mom turns around to look at the TV. She sees bald, naked Larry running through the streets.

She drops her champagne glass on the floor, and then she faints on the couch.

CUT TO:

114. Ext. Downtown Street - Sunrise

There are now hundreds of people shouting and running after Larry.

CROWD

- Catch him!
- Stop him!
- Kill him!

Larry is running for his life and looking exhausted, but then he recognizes something in the distance. It's the drawbridge.

Larry screams.

LARRY

Herbie! Help me! Herbie!

CUT TO:

115. Ext. Drawbridge - Sunrise

Inside the tollbooth, Herbie is wearing the chinchilla hair jacket and humming along to classical music.

Suddenly, he hears the chaos from outside and he springs out of the booth.

He looks towards downtown, and sees the gigantic mob of people yelling and running towards the drawbridge.

Then he spots Larry at the front of the crowd.

Larry screams again.

LARRY
Herbie! Please help me!

HERBIE
Oh my God — LARRY?!
(to himself)
I never thought the day would come when I would use my bridge to separate people, but —
(shouting)
Larry! I'm gonna separate you from that mob!

Herbie pulls the lever inside the booth. The warning buzzer goes off and the lights start flashing. The red and white striped "Danger" plank comes down.

The middle of the drawbridge road slowly splits in half and starts to go up.

HERBIE

Run, Larry, run!

Larry pumps his arms, and he runs as hard and as fast as he can towards the rising drawbridge.

Larry starts to put some distance between himself and the mob. The crowd isn't going to make the drawbridge, but will Larry?

HERBIE

Go Larry! You can make it!

Larry runs up the rapidly growing incline towards the split in the middle of the drawbridge.

The split is growing larger, as the two halves of the drawbridge are moving further apart from one another.

HERBIE

Jump, Larry, jump!

Larry sprints towards the widening gap in the drawbridge, and he leaps across the split.

Larry's naked body sails through the air.

He extends his arms and fingers to try to catch the other side of the drawbridge.

The very tips of Larry's fingers scrape the edge of the other side, but he's not able to grab onto it.

Larry's body plunges towards the water down below.

LARRY

Nooooooooooooooooo!

HERBIE

LARRY!!!

Suddenly, in the blink of an eye, a single strand of thick, green, glowing hair shoots out of Larry's head and grabs onto the edge of the drawbridge.

Larry's body bounces for a moment like he's on the end of a bungee cord, and then the hair swings Larry upwards through the air.

LARRY
Whoaaaaaaaaaaa!

The hair throws Larry onto Herbie's side of the drawbridge, and Larry's body goes tumbling on the cement until his body comes to a stop.

The hair quickly retracts into Larry's scalp and disappears from sight.

Herbie is stunned.

HERBIE
What the heck was that?!

On the other side of the bridge, the mob has stopped running, visibly angry that they couldn't catch Larry.

The hippies throw their knives to the ground in frustration. A man kicks a garbage can. A few people throw their hands up in exasperation.

Herbie looks over at Larry's body lying on the ground. He runs over to Larry.

HERBIE
Oh my God, Larry! Are you okay? What happened to you? Please tell me that you're okay!

Larry slowly stirs on the ground, and then gets to his knees. He stands up and looks a little bit dazed.

Larry slowly looks around.

LARRY

Am I okay?

Larry gives a big grin, and then shouts in glee.

LARRY

Herbie, I'm more than okay! I am fantastic! I've never been better! I'm the luckiest man on the planet, because I'm alive, Herbie! I'm alive! Look at that sunrise! Has the morning sky always been that beautiful? Listen to those birds chirping! They're putting on a concert just for us!

Larry takes in a deep breath through his nose.

LARRY

Can you smell that fresh morning air? There's so much to be grateful for! Herbie, have I ever told you how much I love your cheese?

Larry runs into the booth, grabs some cheese, and pops it into his mouth.

LARRY

Mmmmm... delicious! I gotta get home, Herbie! I'll talk to you soon!

Larry starts running down the street naked.

HERBIE

Wait! Larry! Don't you want to wear something?! Take your coat!

LARRY

It's your coat! I love feeling this cold air on my body! Hee hee hee!

Larry runs off naked into the distance, giggling as he runs.

Herbie looks down at his chinchilla hair jacket with admiration.

HERBIE
I really do love this coat.

DISSOLVE TO:

116. Int. Larry's Bedroom - Night

Larry's mom is tucking Larry into his race car bed. Larry is completely bald.

LARRY
I'm sorry I couldn't beat the curse, mom.

LARRY'S MOM
Oh Larry, I'm just grateful that my little bubala is safe and sound, back at home where you belong.

LARRY
I'm grateful for you too, mom.

She kisses him on the forehead, and walks to the doorway.

LARRY'S MOM
Good night, Larry.

LARRY
Good night.

She turns off the light switch, walks out of the room, and closes the door behind her.

The room is a little darker, but there is a lamp on Larry's nightstand that is still turned on. The lamp has a small chain dangling from it.

Larry is lying in bed with a content smile on his face. He looks over at the lamp, and then his eyeballs shift upwards towards his bald head.

He speaks quietly.

LARRY

Would you mind turning off the light for me?

The single strand of thick, green, glowing hair grows out of Larry's head, reaches over to the lamp, and pulls down on the chain.

CUT TO:

117. Black Screen

Larry speaks in the darkness.

LARRY (O.S.)

Thank you!

THE END

As the closing credits roll, the song "Chinese Translation" by M. Ward plays in the background.

About The Authors

Scott Rose is a software developer, motivational speaker, and Mensa member who loves writing comedy stories and performing both improv & scripted comedy onstage. A self-proclaimed world traveler, he has spent much of his life exploring unfamiliar places. He has lived in 7 cities and has visited 49 countries plus 42 U.S. states — with even more to come. He currently resides in Jacksonville, Florida, although he may have moved by the time you read this, as he continues his pursuit of curiosity and adventure. In the early 2000s, Scott traveled across the United States with the Apple executive team as one of Apple's top professional speakers, and in 2013, Scott went viral with his hit comedy video series "Shit Apple Fanatics Say", which received over 3 million views. His mother, Esther Glickstein Rose, famously named the Big Mac for McDonald's — though Scott now only eats the patties because he is living the keto lifestyle.

Ernie Brandon is a full-time father living in Los Angeles with his wife, daughter, and Rottweiler. He has never met a hobby he didn't like and spends his time juggling an eclectic mix of pursuits: learning foreign languages, creating sketches and illustrations, gardening, cooking, weightlifting, jujitsu, mastering the guitar, conquering video games, and immersing himself in classic films from before the 1980s. He also loves writing short stories and performing onstage in comedic plays.

Scott Rose and Ernie Brandon met while performing improv comedy together in Hollywood. One day, Scott noticed the very beginnings of his hairline receding, when suddenly the book's title popped into his head. He pitched the title to Ernie and asked if he wanted to collaborate on a story based on it. Ernie agreed, and the pair developed the story through countless drafts, late-night discussions, and a noticeable increase in hair loss.

Connect with the authors at:
savinglarryshairline.com

www.ingramcontent.com/pod-product-compliance
Lightning Source LLC
LaVergne TN
LVHW100504110826
845146LV00002B/509

* 9 7 9 8 9 9 4 7 0 2 6 0 4 *